Luke didn't grin back. Pupils blown wide, he stared at her mouth.

From the dim light, surely. It couldn't have anything to do with her.

He cupped her cheek. "Emma..."

Oh. Maybe a little to do with her.

And those fingers, softly tracing her jaw—

She took a deep breath. "I owe you that twenty."

The satisfaction she had expected to see on his face never materialized. He bent his head to hers, lips brushing her temple.

A hint of a touch.

One she could pretend hadn't happened, if she wanted to.

"I thought you looked impressed at one point." His breath warmed her ear. His mouth, too, firmer, nuzzled her cheek.

A thumb stroked the corner of her lips.

Her knees weakened. She slid her palms up his muscled chest. Not for separation. For something to cling to.

Dear Reader,

I'm thrilled to welcome you back to Sutter Creek, especially during the holiday season! *Twelve Dates of Christmas* is the first in a trilogy set at the Moosehorn Wilderness Lodge, a grand, heritage-age mountain getaway with all sorts of romantic possibilities hiding under outdated decor and utilitarian style.

And who better to coax out those charms than ultraromantic Emma Halloran? Of course, her plan to transform the lodge into a luxurious wedding resort is exactly what the current owner's grandson *doesn't* want for the place. When the longtime rivals are put in charge of the lodge's annual Twelve Days of Christmas festival, they clash over everything from geese on the lam to holiday trivia to long-standing family legacies. Luckily for Emma and Luke's happily-ever-after, the festival gives them a dozen opportunities to make Christmas magic—and a dozen opportunities to fall in love!

Keep up to date on new Sutter Creek books and exclusive extras by visiting my website, www.laurelgreer.com, where you'll find the latest news and a link to sign up for my newsletter. I'd love to hear your thoughts on Emma and Luke's story— drop me an email at laurel@laurelgreer.com or come say hello at www.Facebook.com/laurelgreerauthor.

Happy reading!

Laurel

Twelve Dates of Christmas

LAUREL GREER

HARLEQUIN®
SPECIAL EDITION™

ISBN-13: 978-1-335-40817-4

Twelve Dates of Christmas

Copyright © 2021 by Lindsay Macgowan

Harlequin Enterprises ULC
22 Adelaide St. West, 40th Floor
Toronto, Ontario M5H 4E3, Canada
www.Harlequin.com

Printed in U.S.A.

Raised in a small town on Vancouver Island, **Laurel Greer** grew up skiing and boating by day and reading romances under the covers by flashlight at night. Ever committed to the proper placement of the Canadian *eh*, she loves to write books with snapping sexual tension and second chances. She lives outside Vancouver with her law-talking husband and two daughters. At least half her diet is made up of tea. Find her at www.laurelgreer.com.

Books by Laurel Greer

Harlequin Special Edition

Sutter Creek, Montana

From Exes to Expecting
A Father for Her Child
Holiday by Candlelight
Their Nine-Month Surprise
In Service of Love
Snowbound with the Sheriff
Twelve Dates of Christmas

Visit the Author Profile page at Harlequin.com.

For Ellie, who was exceedingly excited
that this book was due on her birthday.
I love how your heart is full of Christmas magic
all year-round, my Bear.

Chapter One

"Holy sh—eet rock, that's hot!" Molten plastic seared Luke Emerson's thumbnail. He dropped his glue gun onto the veranda of his grandfather's wilderness lodge. Yanking at the bead of burning adhesive only smeared it, scorching more of his thumb.

He gritted his teeth, resisting the stinging at the corners of his eyes. This was ridiculous. He could handle pain. A few years back, he'd been winged by a bullet while out in the woods, investigating illegal traps. The next morning, he'd been skulking through the woods, pursuing the less-than-accurate poacher.

Apparently, getting shot in the arm had nothing on branding a thumbnail with crafting glue.

And with six wide-eyed Brownies watching him affix a rainbow of feathers to the gaudiest Christmas tree he'd ever seen, he couldn't even curse away the pain. He shook his hand out until the plastic hardened enough for him to peel it off.

"Are you okay, Mr. Warden?" a pigtailed girl asked. "I can get Ms. Emma. She fixes owies all the—"

"No."

The child startled.

Luke cringed and picked the glue gun up off the wood planking. "Sorry, kiddo, I shouldn't have snapped at you." It wasn't the Brownie's fault the troop leader was a know-it-all who loved to make Luke's blood pressure rise. "I appreciate you trying to help, but I don't need Ms. Emma for this."

He made a point of never needing Emma Halloran for anything.

Thankfully, she'd stopped hovering over his shoulder about ten minutes ago. She was better off over at the beverage table, serving up meticulous portions of hot chocolate to all the tree decorators who needed a warm drink to defrost their fingers. The competition was fierce for the Golden Partridge Award, given out to the winner of the Emerson Wilderness Lodge's annual tree-decorating contest.

The sun had gone down a half hour ago, and the dozen teams were using every second of the final hour in which decorating was allowed. The Twelve Days of Christmas trees anchored the lodge's seasonal festival, one for each verse of the song. They glittered and glowed along the length of the main building's wide porch, festooned with creative interpretations of drummers, geese and golden rings. Starting tonight, Sutter Creek residents would come in droves to vote on the winning tree, participate in twelve days of events and walk the snow-covered light path that meandered through the nearby forest.

He glanced at the drinks table, which was untended. He frowned. Where had Emma gone? Scanning the length of the overhang for her perky brown ponytail, he went to glue another feather on the tree. It landed on his thumb, the knuckle this time.

His eyes crossed and he bit his lip to hold in his shout. He flicked his hand hard enough to make his wrist pang, trying to dislodge the bright pink feather from his skin.

If one more plume stuck to his body, he'd *become* the partridge in the pear tree.

"You need to use your eyeballs, Warden Luke," a skinny, tall-for-her-age munchkin said. Long black twists of hair stuck out under her pink hat.

"That's good advice."

"It's what Ms. Emma always tells us."

Of course it was.

And while he didn't get why the Brownie leader was intent on making the tree into a rainbow bird, he wanted to do right by the kids. The small troop had asked him to help—a request that had earned a storm cloud of a frown from "Ms. Emma"—because he was the tallest person present who wasn't already working on a tree. The girls also seemed to think being the local game warden gave him some sort of magical knowledge about bird-themed crafts.

If feather number one hadn't proved them wrong, feather two sure had.

No matter. He couldn't disappoint the girls, even though he had electrical cords to run, spotlights to position and a staff to organize. And at the top of his to-do list: keep his grandfather from leaving his house to survey the action.

Luke gritted his teeth at the possibility of Hank Emerson trying to hook up the power connections for the trees while hacking up phlegm from his pneumonia-ridden lungs. *No.* Hank was going to keep his stubborn ass fixed to his well-worn couch for the next twelve days, and Luke would do everything else that needed doing.

He got into a rhythm, fully covering the high-up branches the little girls couldn't reach with their shorter arms and rubber cement.

"Now the sparkles." A Brownie peered at him hopefully as she held out a can of spray paint. No, spray *glitter*.

"Your troop leader didn't mention sparkles," he said.

The girl pressed the can into his hand. "We want it on the edges."

"You got it." He was asking for a dressing-down from Emma for following the girls' instructions instead of hers, but she was nowhere to be seen and time was running out. With a careful hand, he sprayed the tips of as many feathers as he could. The Brownies oohed and aahed.

Choking on the fumes, he stepped back, forcing a

straight face as he took in the eyesore. It was a good thing every charity or youth group who entered the twelve-day contest received at least a portion of the total funds raised. If the money was solely awarded to the first-place team, the Brownies wouldn't have a chance at the new canoes they hoped to afford.

The Brownies were clearly of a different mind. They gazed at their creation, faces shining as bright as the pink-and-blue lights Emma had wound through the branches at exact one-inch intervals. Feathers filled in the rest of the spaces. An extra-large papier-mâché pear, wrapped in green, raindrop-size LED bulbs, topped the kaleidoscope monstrosity.

A pear in a partridge tree.

Only Emma...

"Looking great, girls," he lied.

His phone buzzed in his pocket.

A text from his grandpa. How's it coming along?

Luke: Just fine.

Grandpa: I'm feeling better. Need a hand?

God, Grandpa could type fast when he was bored.

Luke glared at his phone and dictated his reply. Come check on things one more time, and I will tie you to your easy chair.

"That's a big frown, Warden Emerson."

The mild comment came from beside him.

He spun, facing Emma Halloran and her glossy red smirk. It didn't matter the occasion—Emma was always done up like she was anticipating an Instagram photoshoot.

And no matter how many times she shot his flannel shirts and muddy work boots a disdainful look, he still struggled to keep his eyes off her. Her wool coat hid the curves of her tall figure, but he'd been able to conjure a mental image of her sexy shape since she sat behind him in twelfth grade English class. He'd turned around so often, trying to bring a blush to her pale cheeks, he'd had to go to the chiropractor for a kink in his neck.

Not much had changed in sixteen years. Not her sleek brown hair begging to be mussed, nor her legs, longer than the Gallatin River.

Nor her love of getting under his skin.

"No one calls me 'Warden' off the job, Emma."

And she knew it.

"Something the matter?" Her eyes glinted, moss-green and curious behind purple plastic glasses.

He shook his head. Emma vibrated with the sort of innate motivation Luke's minor-league hockey coaches had dreamed he'd find somewhere deep within. For all the years Luke had known her, she never seemed to consider the possibility the world wouldn't go her way. Most recently, she'd focused that rose-tinted lens on Emerson Wilderness Lodge.

Not happening. She could take her pie-in-the-sky intention to buy the lodge from his grandfather and shove it. "Everything's fine."

"You sure? You seem stressed." Her smile turned genuine. "I'm happy to help."

More like, happy to take over.

His phone buzzed again, another text from his grandfather. He clenched his jaw. He liked having a beard for several reasons, but at the moment, hiding his irritation ranked high.

"See," she said. "Something's not right."

He sighed. She played cribbage with his grandfather every Monday night. Though Luke questioned her motives for the ongoing arrangement—it had to have something to do with her intention to buy the lodge—she'd been legitimately upset over the older man's illness. "Grandpa's trying to convince me that three days of antibiotics have cured him, and he should be down here stringing lights."

Emma's dark brows drew together. "He did not."

He showed her the screen.

"For crying out loud," she said. "I'll go talk to him. He isn't contagious anymore, is he?"

"He isn't. But don't worry about it. I think he listened to me."

A faint cough rattled from the direction of the cabins.

"Or not," Emma said.

Luke groaned, peering toward his grandfather's one-bedroom cottage. The lights of the front window made a halo around Hank Emerson's uncharacteristically stooped shoulders.

"You have a mighty interesting definition of 'listened,'" Emma said.

He opened his mouth, scrambling for a retort as

the porch lights suddenly went out, blanketing the crowd in darkness.

What the hell?

Six Brownie squeals rent the air, along with a cacophony of confusion from the decorating teams. Another cough sounded from the direction of Hank's cottage.

Luke craned his neck. Everything was shadowed in dark gray, except for the three streetlights illuminating the overflow parking lot two hundred yards to the east and the glow from the guest cabins in the distance. He could barely see the people around him, let alone monitor what Hank was doing.

"What's happening?" someone called out from the other end of the veranda.

"Probably a fuse! Give me a minute to figure it out," he shouted back.

Emma sprang to action rounding up her charges, reassuring them the lights would come back on soon and everyone would get to see their pretty tree.

As if that's the priority.

Except it was, to a large extent. His grandfather had been musing about retirement. And with Hank having refused Luke's offer to take over running the lodge on a permanent basis, Luke needed to do what he could to ensure the Emerson name stayed on the sign he'd helped Hank build out by the main road. If the festival flopped, or if Emma interfered too much, his grandpa might take those musings and turn them into reality.

"Luke!" The operations manager's voice came

through the darkness. She carried an industrial-size flashlight. "We're having a problem with the electrical. Not the fuses. I checked them."

"And the generator?" Luke asked.

The lodge's chef was hot on his coworker's heels. "Generator's not going to reach out here."

Awesome.

"Then let's try to—"

His cell rang. He glanced at the screen. The sheriff. Concern crept up the back of his neck. Was there more to the power outage than aging wiring?

"It's Sheriff Rafferty, excuse me," he said to the crowd starting to gather around him. He answered the call. "Hello?"

"Emerson, you still on the clock, or should I be calling whoever's filling in for you on your vacation?" Ryan Rafferty asked in his usual no-nonsense tone.

Fish, Wildlife and Parks business, then. "I'm off tomorrow, and for a week starting Friday. Working today, though," he said. He'd requested his vacation time months ago, only taking two days off during the first week of the festival. But with his grandpa sick, he wished he'd booked all twelve days, not the patchwork arrangement he'd made. Evening and weekend calls were part of the job, so he couldn't guarantee he'd be around for Wednesday's "Three French Hens" chicken dinner or Thursday's "Four Calling Birds" animal call competition.

"Hate to interrupt your evening, but I got a call about suspicious lights over by RG Ranch."

"Maybe they'd be so kind as to bring them over here," he joked. "Our main building lost power a few minutes ago."

Rafferty swore. "Sorry, I need to pull you away. I'm not sure if this is connected to last year's cattle thefts or if someone's spotlighting for deer. I'd like you there if it's the latter."

Hunting out of season *and* using illegal lights? Heat singed his belly. If his job had taught him one thing, it was that people were stupid enough to try anything. "I'll meet you over there. I'll leave in five, after I make sure everything's safe here."

They arranged a meeting place and hung up.

He ran a hand down his face, smoothing his beard. A headache blossomed at his temples. The minute Hank found out Luke had to leave, he'd start poking around, trying to solve the lighting issue on the heritage-age building.

He looked at the ops manager and the chef. "I'm going to need an hour or two," he said. "Are you going to be able to deal with the electrical issues without me?"

"We'll try," the ops manager said. "I—"

His grandfather's growly cough echoed down the overhang. "Did someone check the breakers?"

"Grandpa! We've got this. You need to rest," Luke said.

"I'll rest when the power's back on." A deep, rumbling hack punctuated the claim.

"We're not done with our tree!" someone shouted

from a few yards down. Others added their complaints.

Luke's eyes were adjusting to the dim, far-off streetlights, and the crowd of people looked less than impressed. The band of tension tightened around his head. "Let me think—"

"Oh, good grief," came Emma's voice from near his shoulder. "Would you let me help, already?" She cleared her throat and held out her hand for the ops manager's flashlight. "Listen up!"

She waved her hands, and the crowd calmed. "All of you, sit tight. We can extend the decorating time by however many minutes we lose waiting for the power to come back on. We'll bribe any early crowds with free hot chocolate and cookies while they wait."

He hated giving Emma any credit, not when it was obvious she was pitching in to further ingratiate herself with his grandfather. But a time extension was a simple, smart solution. The crowd grumbled in reluctant agreement with her compromise.

"Well, hold on now." Hank turned around, coughing violently.

Luke rushed over to his grandfather, holding the older man's elbow. "Easy, Grandpa. Giving out free cookies is a small price to pay."

"Graydon!" Emma called out for her younger brother, a firefighter with the Sutter Creek department who was decorating the tree with a lords a-leaping theme at the other end of the overhang. "You and your crew can help out with the wiring. We need lights if we're going to run this event."

"Hang on," Luke protested. "You don't get to make those kinds of decisions."

Glancing at him like he had as many loose screws as the rainbow tree had ugly feathers, she addressed the grandmotherly woman who had been hanging crocheted turtledoves on the adjacent noble fir. "Gail, do you mind watching these lovely ladies for ten minutes?"

"Of course not."

"Thanks." She leaned down to her Brownies' level. "Sweethearts, wait right here for a few minutes, okay? I'm going to go with Mr. Emerson to see if he has any extra flashlights." Emma took Hank by his other elbow. "You, sir, are a menace," she said in an affectionate whisper. "You can either walk back to that cabin with your head held high, or I'll play your crutch the whole way there. What's your choice?"

Hank didn't answer, just coughed and started to make his way slowly along the path.

She cocked her head at Luke. "Doesn't the sheriff need you? I'll make sure everything goes off without a hitch."

He knew she would.

He didn't have to like it, even if he did need the help tonight.

"Don't get any ideas, Emma," he warned.

"Like what?" she murmured under her breath.

"Trying to convince Grandpa to accept that asinine purchase offer you made." Hank had put too much of himself into the lodge, had created too much of an environmental legacy on the property, to sell it back to the granddaughter of the previous owners.

"I'm here to decorate a Christmas tree with *children*, Luke," she said. "If I happen to be able to put my event planning expertise to use for the night, it'll only be to your benefit."

His stomach ground at the truth of her statement. "I'll be back as soon as I can."

She waved a hand. "Take your time."

"Not likely." He pivoted on a boot heel and headed for his truck. He wasn't letting her oversee the festival for a minute longer than necessary. She needed to understand that the Emerson Wilderness Lodge was going to stay under Emerson management.

Emma tucked a knitted blanket around Hank's lanky frame and turned on his television. "What's your pleasure? Romance, or classic?"

"I recorded the new royal holiday movie. Pull that up, if you would."

She smiled, loving how the older man was as much of a sucker for seasonal films as Emma was herself.

She found the recording and passed him the remote. "There. If you want to watch something festive tonight, it's going to exist on a screen."

She kept her voice firm even though his raspy breathing sent jolts of fear through her. Hank had been her grandfather's best friend. She hated seeing illness zap his energy and vitality. His usually tanned skin was way too pasty for her liking. "If you don't get better, we won't be able to play cards on Monday."

After her grandparents' fatal car accident a few years back, she'd started playing weekly cribbage with Hank in Grammy and Gramps's stead. They'd grieved together, her whole purpose of maintaining the tradition, but all the time on Hank's front porch had turned into something unexpected, as well. Hours and hours watching the seasons change around the rough-hewn, log-sided lodge had tugged at her.

Luke was right—she *did* want to own this property, to restore the glorified fishing resort to the luxurious, romance-focused retreat it had been before her grandparents had sold it to Hank. Her great-grandfather had constructed most of the buildings on the property, and that history dwelled in her DNA. A photo album of couples enjoying dance classes, movie nights and string-quartet dinners sat on her shelf in her apartment, nagging her to bring it back to life.

Even better, to add her own ideas, and offer full wedding services.

With the correct care and attention, it could be done. Not Luke's stubborn insistence he knew what was best, even as the lodge fell to pieces.

This wasn't the time to be worrying about that, though. She had an equally stubborn Emerson to deal with.

Hank watched the movie with a melancholy smile. "Everything okay?"

He paused the recording. "Thinking of Jenny."

Emma gave him a hug. His late wife had been a dynamo, much like her Grammy.

"I feel like I'm letting her down. She lived for this festival. Can't stand being useless." He hacked into the crook of his elbow. "Who knows how long Luke's call will take?"

"I've dealt with bigger surprises at the resort." She'd worked for her uncle's ski resort since college, shifting from event planning to the development team to marketing over the years. And once she convinced Hank to accept her offer, she'd need every ounce of experience she'd gleaned to transform the lodge. "It's all under control."

"Thanks, darlin'."

"My pleasure." Excitement ran through her. Making sure things went well for the festival's "first day of Christmas" would help Hank and Luke relax and would be a heck of a lot of fun.

She brought Hank a mug of peppermint tea from his kitchen. "Need anything else?"

"Yeah, to get off this couch."

"Sorry. Not happening," she said cheerfully.

"You're a mean nurse, Emma Halloran. You and Luke sure are a pair."

Emma's mouth flattened. She and Luke were too different to be a pair. Opposites attract was a myth, a guaranteed heartbreak. She'd been looking for "the one" since high school, and she'd only gotten close to forever with men who shared her interests and goals.

Not Luke Emerson, even if their opinions on Hank's health matched.

"Someone needs to boss you around sometimes," she teased. "I'd better get back to my minions. I mean, my Brownies."

"Feels like yesterday it was you in the brown uniform, with Winnie as the troop leader," Hank mused. "Nice that you've kept up her tradition."

"Best role model I could ask for." She kissed the top of his head and pointed at the coffee table. "Tea, inhaler, phone—you're set. Text if you need something, okay?"

He nodded sharply and pressed Play on the remote. Generic, holiday-esque instrumental music tinkled from the TV.

"Let me know if it's good," she said. "It's on my to-watch list."

"Stay and keep me company," Hank said.

"Another day. I need to go save your grandson's bacon." Winking at him, she jogged out into the cold.

Her heeled boots weren't the most practical for speeding down a snowy path, but she had work to do. Getting the lights on, for starters. The space was still dark. Echoey complaints filtered through the night air from the restless tree decorators. And her Brownies... *Shoot.* They had to be her priority, as well as the lighting.

She called out for calm, quelling the muttering. She'd ensure her girls were safely back in their parents' care, then deal with the unhappy crowd.

"The tree is stunning, girls," she said. The troop clustered around the feathery pièce de résistance. Two of them held flashlights. "Thanks for staying put. Your parents should be here to pick you up any minute."

"Ms. Emma, I don't like the dark."

And Emma didn't like the way Addie's lip was casting wobbly shadows on the girl's light brown face. She knelt in front of the child. "The dark makes it easier to see the stars. You're safe, honey."

Two poufs of hair bobbed in concert with a sniffle. "Okay."

"Was Warden Emerson super helpful with the feathers?" Emma asked.

"He burned himself, like, ten times." Cammie, Addie's twin, fidgeted with one of her hair twists.

Emma held in a snort. *So much for "anyone can handle gluing," hey, Luke?*

"He almost swore, too," Cammie added. She shone her flashlight at the top branches. "He made the feathers look pretty, though."

"It looks fantastic," Emma said.

Cammie's beam was incandescent; Addie's smile was watery. Identical appearances, but wholly different personalities. Emma felt that deeply—she was nothing like her own siblings.

Graydon. Right. She needed to check in with the firefighters and the lodge employees and see if they'd figured out the source of the power outage.

She opened her brother's text thread and typed, How long until this is fixed?

His reply came after a few seconds. Patience.

She made a face at the screen. Patience was overrated. *He's doing his best. Luke is, too.*

A few minutes later, the girls' parents showed up, and she was Brownie-free and able to investigate the power outage and get the rest of the crowd settled down.

It took the maintenance crew about ten more minutes to fix the wiring on the electrical panel. With the trees now illuminated and glittering, she announced to the decorating teams that they had an extra half hour to finish their creations.

Okay, cookies, hot chocolate, check with the parking lot crew, make sure signage is in place...

She grinned to herself. For every problem she addressed, it got that much easier to picture herself in this role for good. Not only following in her grandparents' footsteps, but finally finding a place for herself, too.

Chapter Two

Emma spent the next thirty minutes speeding around the veranda and the adjacent snow-covered path, making sure all the lodge employees knew what they were doing and had everything they needed to make opening night as magical as possible. She handed out refreshments to early arrivals and kept the foot traffic flowing once the viewing area opened. Two hours passed before she got a moment to grab a warm beverage of her own, stand back and appreciate the sight of guests having fun in an orderly, well-organized manner.

Which is exactly what I want for this place.

The bones of the building were gorgeous—soaring ceilings, a stunning river-rock fireplace, intimate nooks for romance. It just needed some glamor to complement the rustic beauty. And she loved Hank, but the Twelve Days of Christmas festival was as romantic as the place ever got these days. The activities were usually all fishing and hunting and wilderness adventures.

Fine, for some. Not for Emma, if she had her way and turned it into a destination.

She envisioned one thousand percent more tasteful wall sconces and chandeliers, one thousand percent fewer decorative antlers and stuffed fish. Nostalgic odes to Grammy's classic style, nestled in Emma's own modern design.

"They have you on the payroll now?" Graydon teased, sidling up to her. Where Emma had dark hair and her mom's thin frame, Graydon was blond and bulky. He'd been a bruiser of a defenseman when he played hockey in high school.

Like Luke had been fifteen years earlier. She'd known then they had nothing in common, and he wasn't anywhere close to the perfect love her grandmother had promised Emma would find one day. Even so, she'd had to force herself not to stare at him as he flew around the ice during games.

Growling at the mental image of teenage Luke Emerson in thick hockey pads, hair curling at the back of his helmet, she shook her head. "They're shorthanded with Hank out sick."

"Gonna take a while for Hank to recover. Pneumonia's a bitch." Gray sipped from his paper cup.

"True. And I don't think he's going to relax while the festival's going on."

They'd probably need extra help all week. She was pretty sure Luke was taking time off to fill in for his grandpa for part of the festival, but if this afternoon had proved anything, he'd be out of his element.

Emma knew she would be the opposite. And she was also on vacation from now until Christmas...

"If I pitched in for the rest of the festival, it might encourage Hank to relax," she told her brother. *Maybe I could use the time to get through Luke's hard skull, too.*

Gray blinked at her. "Hell of a way to spend your holidays."

"Worth it, though."

"Mom'll flip out if you miss any family Christmas stuff."

"'Flip out' is a bit of an overstatement," she said. If Gray wasn't there, yeah, their mom would be upset. He was the baby of the family by a decade, the precious surprise.

He had his place amongst the Halloran siblings. *And me? I'm still looking for mine.*

She wasn't the ranching expert like her oldest sister, or a smoke-jumping hero like her cousin Jack, who'd lived with them since he was a kid. Or even the family rebel like her younger sister, Bea. Third-best, middle-of-the-pack Emma.

Her grandparents had been the ones to understand her more than anyone in the family. She'd never had to fight to get noticed by Grammy and Gramps. Not only had they been wonderful role models for what a relationship should look like, but they'd also always seen her, understood her.

She doubted she'd ever manage to stand out amongst her siblings, but she *could* create a place for herself on this property. She needed to turn the lodge into something as romantic and long-lasting as Grammy and Gramps's fifty-year marriage.

It made business sense, too. Focusing on marketing it as a wedding venue and couples' retreat would get it noticed in an area of Montana that already had a successful, high-end resort. A half hour later she was finishing up the donation count for the night when she glimpsed Luke striding along the path from the parking lot. He still wore jeans, but he'd put on his bulletproof vest and utility belt at some point. His winter uniform jacket hung open across his chest.

Something pulsed at her core.

For crying out loud. Nothing pulsed. No. Thing.

She was not attracted to Luke. Especially not all uniformed up as a warden. Body armor and belts full of weapons and tools had never been her thing.

He joined her at her table and examined the thinning crowd with his usual intent gaze. He jerked his head in greeting. "Emma."

"How'd the search go?" she asked.

He lifted a broad shoulder. "No illegal activity in the area from what I could see. Saw your mom, though. She says hi."

"You were at the ranch?"

"Your mom was the one who called in the report. I hear she's been twitchy since the thefts."

"Of course she has been," Emma snapped. Recently solved cattle thefts had bitten into her parents' ranch's bottom line, big-time. Emma was lucky her inheritance was sufficient for a down payment on the lodge and that her uncle had offered to be her guarantor on her future mortgage. Her parents were in no place to help her make her dream a reality right now.

Luke held up his hands. "As she should be, firecracker."

"*Firecracker?* Are you kidding me?"

His mouth twitched. "Little bit."

Ugh, why did she always let him nettle her? Having grown up as his neighbor—Hank's land bordered the west side of her family's ranch—she should be immune to those teasing smiles. Luke and his mom had lived in the cottage next to Hank's from Luke's elementary school years until he moved to Oregon for his flash-in-the-pan moment in professional hockey.

The early-morning school bus rides and being in the same grade had never translated into him being her friend, though. He'd made it clear she drove him bananas.

She crossed her arms. "Tonight went well, in case you care. Donations flowed in. People were loving the trees and the cookies."

"I care. A lot." His face was cast in shadow, darkening his gray eyes to charcoal. His thick beard covered his sharp jawline, framed his white-edged lips. Strong cheekbones, nose a little crooked from when he broke it snowboarding in tenth grade. God, he'd milked that injury, strutting through the halls like his two black eyes made him a hero.

And she'd fallen for it. Had forced herself to be extra snippy to hide how much she hated seeing him hurt.

"I care, too," she said, pushing the memory aside.

"Not for the same reason."

"For the *exact* same reason." She put her hands on her hips. "I'm worried about Hank."

"And you want to interfere with the lodge."

"Not interfere. Buy. Rejuvenate. Transform. Pick a verb."

"How about *happen*. As in *not going to*." The words came out low, the tone gritty. "I will not let you erase everything my grandpa's done for conservation in the area by catering to spoiled brides and grooms."

Good grief. He was like one of the precious fish he adored catching—a person needed to play with the line, let him swim out a little, before reeling him in. She'd have to start small, prove herself invaluable for one activity and *then* insist he needed her for all twelve days. And by the end of that, she'd prove to him her vision was just as valid as the lodge's current reality.

"What's tomorrow's event—something to do with turtledoves?" she said.

"Snow-shelter building competition."

Snow shelters? That sounded…cold.

Sure, she worked for a ski resort, but because she loved maximizing guest experiences, not because she enjoyed the weather. Ah, well. She could wear the gear she pulled out the couple times a year she did winter activities with her Brownie troop.

"What do forts have to do with turtledoves?" she asked.

"They're nesting birds," he said, talking to her as if she was a toddler. "Nests, shelters for two... It's close enough. Lovey-dovey. Right up your alley."

"Squishing into a frigid snow fort is not 'lovey-dovey.'"

He lifted an eyebrow. "You'd know better than I would."

"What's that supposed to mean?"

"You're always dating someone."

"Geez, judgy much?"

"I'm a realist, Emma," he said. "Relationships aren't worth the trouble."

Well, that was plain sad. She'd spent many a tea-time talking with her grandmother about what to look for in a partner. Luke got a big strike-through on Grammy's most important piece of advice: find someone open to love and all its possibilities.

"How can you be sure?" she said. "It's been what, over a decade since you dated someone for longer than a week? You have to actually *try* something to know whether it's worth it or not. And falling in love... It's like the sun's shining directly on you and the person you're with. It's being understood and seen and finding your place in someone else's heart—" Not that she'd had that with the last few men she'd committed to, but it was always worth the attempt.

"Are you trying to convince me, or yourself?" he murmured.

She wanted to wipe the skepticism off his face with one of her fluffy, pale pink mittens. "What time does everything start tomorrow? I'll be here."

"To build snow forts?" he said, voice rising with incredulity.

"You think I can't?"

He crossed his arms over his chest.

Wow. That was a good look for him, jacketed muscles hard and strong over the khaki green of his service vest. Plus the protective, conscientious nature that went along with being game warden—

Look away. Now.

Before her desire to find love had her seriously considering a man who didn't want a relationship *and* was determined to block her dream of owning the lodge.

But the tingles in her chest when she was around him… She hadn't felt those in a long time.

It's irritation, not *attraction.*

"You're not exactly one with the outdoors," he said.

There. That. Focus on his disdain.

"You don't know everything about me," she said.

"I know plenty about you."

Argh, his quiet confidence made her blood boil. Didn't need to worry about staying warm in the

December cold when Luke Emerson was around to make her feel like she was sitting in a sauna.

"I can be valuable, even building snow forts. Let me prove it to you."

"It's a midday activity," he said. "Aren't you working?"

"Not between now and Christmas." Sutter Creek never lacked for holiday fun, and this year would be extra special because her sister would be in town as of Thursday. "I always take these two weeks off to make sure I have time for all the festive traditions."

"Lucky me," he said under his breath.

She poked him in the biceps. Those hard-as-a-rock biceps… "You're a crappy whisperer."

"I can whisper fine when I feel like it." His voice lowered into dirty territory.

Mmm. Luke's whisper, brushing across the sensitive skin of her ear…

She swallowed, trying to keep her mouth from drying out. "Why are you saying no to another set of hands?"

Unless he disliked her just that much. The possibility stung more than she wanted to admit.

He scrubbed his palm over his face. "I don't know. I'll need the help to wrangle my grandpa, if nothing else. So if you want to pitch in tomorrow, I'll see you at eight a.m." His gaze dragged from her coat to her jeans and leather boots. "Dress for the elements. We need to build an example shelter before the competition starts."

"What, I shouldn't wear my couture, Luke? Shocking."

"You're…" He frowned and waved a hand at her clothes. "Fancy. You know what I mean."

"I know you're condescending. But I'm still going to help you. I can handle the cold. *And* you." She shoved the cash box at him and headed for her car, his chuckle echoing behind her.

Eight sharp for fort building? Give her an hour for internet research when she got home tonight, and she'd build the best freaking snow shelter he'd ever seen.

Her dream depended on it.

She wanted to make magic for couples, start off their lives together with a day where everything was exactly how they wanted it. For herself, too, one day. She'd been picturing getting married on the beautiful deck overlooking the river since she was a little girl dressing up in Grammy's wedding veil.

Eventually, she'd find a man willing to stand up with her and match her promise of forever.

A man *nothing* like Luke Emerson.

Luke walked past the decorated trees on the porch at seven fifteen the next morning, his heavy snow boots echoing off the wood planking. Arriving at the lodge forty-five minutes early would allow him to get organized and be completely in control by the time Emma arrived.

She had a longer commute than he did, driving in from town. Luke only had to shuffle down the path from the cabins. He'd been staying at the lodge for his Christmas holidays for years now. Years ago, when he'd slunk back to Montana from Oregon, his grandfather had offered him one of the bigger cabins to live in. Luke had declined, knowing his monthly rent wouldn't be near what his grandpa would make from daily or weekly tourist rates. But he did take the older man up on the offer for two weeks a year during the holiday extravaganza.

Aside from ensuring the snow-shelter competition went off without a hitch, he had one job today: keep an eye on Emma and stop her from getting her dreamy, I-have-a-plan glint in her eyes.

When Hank had first mentioned retirement but had refused Luke's offer to take over running the place, it had been like getting beaned in the head with a slap shot. *Doesn't line up with your skill set, son.*

Hard not to take that personally. He'd worked his ass off in college, managing his dyslexia and getting his natural resource management degree after being dropped by his pro team. But Hank was convinced Luke would be miserable running a business. Too bad he didn't have an MBA like Emma's... Not that her expensive piece of paper meant she understood that people came back to the lodge year after year to enjoy hearty food and time in the outdoors with family and friends, not to be pampered and fed microgreens.

And weddings? They'd had the occasional ceremony during his grandfather's ownership. Switching focus entirely, and losing the commitment to environmental preservation, would be devastating to the river and surrounding wilderness.

Luke jogged under the portico and through the front doors, belly churning with the need to preserve his grandfather's efforts.

Whenever the wood-paneled, high-ceilinged space was decorated for Christmas it never failed to remind Luke of awkward childhood pictures of him and his cousin Brody dressed in turtlenecks under matching red sweaters. Touches of his grandmother's vintage gold tinsel glittered in the windows, and a live Christmas tree stood in a place of honor between faded plaid couches. Only the front desk lacked a strong retro vibe. He and his grandfather had designed and crafted the pine behemoth with wood they'd milled themselves. He wasn't going to be modest—the piece was gorgeous.

And Emma was leaning against it like a model hawking snow gear in some upscale European ski magazine.

Also gorgeous. And *early.*

Damn it.

She was facing away from him, seemingly focused on something down the hall. Her long dark hair was pulled back in some sort of intricate French braid.

"I thought I said eight," he said.

She didn't turn.

He approached, thinking he'd catch her attention from the side. A pair of white AirPods were lodged in her delicate ears. She was staring at the brown carpeting at the other end of the foyer like she wanted to light it on fire with her eyes.

She probably did. He'd bet all the cash in his wallet Emma had started a "things to change" list months ago. It no doubt started with "rip up the flooring."

"Emma," he said, raising his voice.

She jolted and removed her headphones. "Oh! Luke. Sorry. I didn't see you. I was finishing up a marketing podcast."

"Before eight on a Tuesday?"

"We can't all be addicted to hip waders and glacier-fed creeks," she said.

He couldn't deny fishing was his preferred escape from life. And her snarky opinion about it was no surprise. The one time he'd invited her out to the river, she'd turned him down with a stellar eye roll. Sure, that had been when they were teens, but in the years since he'd never noticed her taking advantage of the pristine wilderness around Sutter Creek. She was more about chatting at Peak Beans or going to karaoke night at the Loose Moose.

He motioned to her headphones. "Aren't you supposed to be on vacation?"

She narrowed her eyes. "I enjoy what I do."

"So why do you want to buy this place so badly?" He had not had enough coffee to properly maneuver through a conversation with Emma Halloran. "You could be set for life at Sutter Mountain, working for your uncle."

She blinked at him and returned her AirPods to their shiny case. "The truth? It's hard to stand out in my family. Working for my uncle makes it worse. I want something that's both connected to my roots *and* that's mine."

She smiled. Not calculated, like he'd have thought, but sweet and open.

"I'll have to show you," she said. "Later. We have a snow fort to build."

"A snow *shelter*," he grumbled. "After coffee."

"Oh! I got you one." She held out a large to-go cup sporting the Peak Beans logo on the cardboard sleeve. "I ordered it extra hot. Should still be drinkable."

He took it. The warmth from the cup soaked through his glove. "Thank you."

"It's black, like your anti-romance heart."

Midsip, he spluttered.

Her face was all feigned innocence. She pulled a tissue from her pocket and handed it to him.

Those eyes, green and clear like the center of a river when the sun shot through it on an angle—

Argh. Not something he needed to be noticing about Emma Halloran.

She reached into the pocket of her parka again. The material was fitted at the waist, luring him to test the shape with a hand—

"Luke?"

He focused on her suspicious expression. "Yeah?"

"I *said*, I have a plan."

"Do you, now?"

"Of course I do. Nothing gets me going more than a plan."

He almost choked on his tongue. "Lists are your foreplay?"

Pink bloomed on her cheeks. "No!"

Maybe she'd never let anyone break through all her rigid expectations to leave her in pretty, sated disarray. Maybe Luke could—

No. He would never be that man.

It'd be the epitome of selfishness, given his track record of letting down the people he loved.

He forced a teasing smile. "Must be quite the plan."

She flattened the sheet of paper on the pine top of the front desk. "It is. I sketched a blueprint."

He raised his eyebrows. "You didn't think I'd have a design in mind?"

"You don't like this one?" Straight white teeth worried her plush, raspberry-glossed lip. Would she taste sweet, like stealing summer berries off the vine?

He shook the fantasy from his head and glanced over the arches and shelves of her design. "That's a ton of digging. It's easier to use the method I already know."

"Oh. Of course." She folded up the sketch. The disappointment on her face would have felled a water buffalo, let alone one grown-ass man.

"I usually do a T shape," he explained. "It's faster."

"Isn't it supposed to be turtledove themed? *Couple* themed? Wouldn't it make more sense to have a single sleeping platform inside? To share, instead of being on separate benches."

He sighed. Did it really matter, provided they got it built on time? "Sure. It isn't like you and I have to actually use the thing."

She bristled. "Ouch."

"I didn't mean—"

"Yeah, you did." She tossed back the rest of her coffee and dropped the cup and lid into the recycling and organics holes in the lobby's wood-topped garbage container. Her cheeks were pink again. Was she legit bothered by the thought of him not wanting to share a snow cave with her?

He'd always assumed he'd fail to clear Emma's sky-high bar, so he'd never bothered to try. Living up to the expectations of practical folks was hard enough. He'd struggled with it all his life. Teachers, hockey coaches, his grandfather... They'd all dreamed big alongside him, wanting him to go pro, follow in his grandfather's footsteps.

In failing out of hockey in a spectacular fashion, Luke had wasted their precious time and effort *and* crushed the future he and his fiancée had intended to build. The headlines still flashed in his head some nights, keeping him awake.

The Emerson Embarrassment.

Golden Grandson? Try Groans, Son.

All Skates, No Smarts.

He swallowed a lump of shame. "We need to start out at the toolshed—we'll tow the shovels and other supplies out to the parking lot with Grandpa's snow-mobile."

"The parking lot?" Emma tilted her head in confusion.

"We dig the shelters there—along the backside of the berm that's built up from clearing snow off the asphalt. We'll tape off the areas for each of the twelve teams, set out the starting area with shovels, tools. The central tent is for the PA, Christmas music, first aid… More hot chocolate and coffee, as well as the propane heaters and barrels for anyone who comes to watch."

"All right," she said, smile stiff. "Put me to work."

Chapter Three

Luke could say one thing about digging a livable space into the ten-foot-high snowbank nearest the competition's tent—as long as he focused on turfing heavy shovelfuls out the three-square-foot entrance, he could ignore how the cozy dome smelled like Emma's sweet-tart shampoo.

Sort of ignore.

All right, fine—not at all.

About fifteen minutes into their task, he'd figured out she washed her hair with something scented like a sugar-crusted lemon grove. Now they were at the two-hour mark of bumping into each other and shoveling elbow to elbow. Tonight, he'd no doubt dream of his favorite kind of pie, sunshine-yellow custard topped with fluffy, toasted meringue.

Or dream of licking that custard off Emma's skin.

Icy blue light glowed through the snow above their heads. They had the dome carved out and were finishing up making the three-tiered design. She kneeled on the top shelf, smoothing out the sleeping platform with her hands. With every movement, her snow pants tightened against her curves.

Every muscle in his body tightened, too. He'd forced himself to ignore Emma in fussy little skirts and painted-on jeans since freshman year. Go figure that black Gore-Tex and a pair of Sorels were his downfall.

Hell. He lived next to a damn mountain. Attractive women wore ski gear in Sutter Creek all the time. He was all for looking—and maybe doing a bit more—so long as they were good with keeping things light. He'd had enough of being a disappointment.

Cursing under his breath, he focused on chiseling out the bottom level with his shovel.

"Why is this not getting *level*?" Emma complained. "I need tools. One of those flatheaded, paint scraper thingies. But giant."

His mouth twitched. "A joint knife."

"Do you have one?"

"Nope." He sat back on his heels. "No tools except shovels, hands and anything you can find in the woods."

"Who made that rule?"

"Me."

"When?"

"Three seconds ago."

She threw a handful of snow at him. "You're such a pain!"

And you're too easy to rile.

He wiped the icy dots from his face with the sleeve of his jacket. "It's not going to be slide-rule accurate. We don't have time."

"People are going to see it, though."

He separated his glove from his sleeve with a thumb and finger to check his watch. "They'll start showing up in twenty minutes."

She growled, a sweet little sound of frustration. "This is the exemplar. It should be perfect. We haven't even had the chance to add any romantic details yet."

"Emma," he said. "No one's coming for that. They just want to enjoy the sunshine, drink free cocoa and watch Aleja Brooks Flores win like she has for the last ten years."

She crossed her arms. "There's always room for romance."

Not in Luke's experience. "You live in quite the fantasy world."

She stiffened. "What could you possibly know about my fantasies?"

Not enough.

"Nothing. Nor do I want to." Figuring out Emma Halloran was beyond him. "I know enough about your realities. You romanticize the hell out of life. You've told half the eligible men around our age in Sutter Creek that you love them."

Fury flashed in her eyes. "You're judging the number of men I've dated?"

Crap. That had come out wrong. "No. God, no. Date who you want, whenever you want. But I know you've been in relationships with some of my friends, and there's no way you actually fell in love with all of them."

"What, you're all sitting around taking notes?" She jammed her hand shovel into the back wall a few times. "Comparing Emma's-an-evil-witch stories?"

"No, but guys do discuss their girlfriends now and again. And I have a good memory."

Her only response was a few scoops of snow pitched on his lap.

"Careful," he said. "We're probably deep enough into the berm."

"The bed needs to be bigger."

"Not really."

She sent him a glare. "It's better to at least try to find love than to sit and sulk for years."

"Who's sulking?"

"You are, ever since you moved back from Oregon."

Heat tore up the back of his neck. It would be a waste of breath to try to convince her he was better off alone. "No, I was focusing on work. Putting my nose to the grindstone. Unlike you, I couldn't depend on family connections to get me my job."

"Excuse me? I got my job on my own merit." The tips of her ears turned bright pink. She reached a few feet up and drove the blade into the wall.

"Wait, Emma, don't dig so close to the—"

Snow tumbled down around her head.

She screamed and scrambled back.

Luke grabbed her around the waist and yanked her toward the entrance.

Thwomp.

Snow cascaded over his lower legs. Sun pierced his vision.

Relief swamped him, making his head spin. He'd managed to get them half in, half out of the shelter, wedged together in the opening. He inhaled the crisp air. Emma nestled against his chest, body vibrating in his arms. Her panting breaths pelted his neck.

"H-holy—"

"Shh." He tightened his grip on her shaking shoulders. "We're okay."

"We're stuck!"

Her frustrated, fear-ridden cry echoed off the nearby trees.

"I don't think we are." He kicked at the snow. With some effort, he managed to free his legs. "Move your feet. It didn't collapse the whole way."

"It could have landed on *me*."

"It didn't."

A squeaky whimper escaped her.

"You're safe." He forced a calm tone. His pulse hammered in his chest and his ears.

"Thank you." Her forehead dropped to the notch at the base of his neck.

It would be so easy to drop a kiss to the top of her head, for no other reason than to soothe her…

No. Holding her was enough.

"Time to move, firecracker."

The nickname seemed to do the trick. She wiggled.

Wiggled against *him*.

Focus, Emerson. On getting them unstuck, not on Emma's soft body and the cloud of sweet citrus filling his nose. "That's right. You got it. Once we get our feet free, we can push off, scooch out together."

Damp, shock-filled green eyes stared up at him. "Is *scooch* a technical term?"

"It is today."

Her jaw set. "When I own this place, we will not be building snow shelters."

Her words landed on his chest like another load of snow. "We're not talking about that now."

Jogging footsteps thumped toward them. A curse rent the air. "Luke? *Emma?*"

"Gray?" Emma called out.

Emma's brother knelt in the snow next to them. A small crowd of employees and guests followed close behind. Concern flashed across the firefighter's face. "Are either of you hurt? What the hell happened?"

Luke glanced down at Emma. Her face flamed red. Half of him appreciated the rescue. The other half was annoyed he couldn't stay cozied up in the snow with Emma. And all of him wanted to save her the embarrassment of admitting she'd been at fault for the collapse.

"My bad, Halloran," Luke said to Graydon. "Got too close to the surface."

"What?" Confusion muddied Emma's gaze. "But I—"

He hugged her tighter.

"Want to help us out?" Luke asked the brawny firefighter.

Gray grabbed Luke under the arms and started pulling. Luke braced his boots against the wall of snow inside and pushed with his legs.

Goddamn, it *had* almost landed on Emma...

An aftershock of fear ripped through him, jacking his pulse higher.

It only took seconds to free them. Emma sprang to her feet, brushing off her coat, face pink and expression prim.

Grinning, Luke spread-eagled in the snow, trying to shift the crowd's attention onto him alone.

"That, folks, is why we get everyone to sign a waiver."

"You and Luke, huh?"

Emma broke away from the glorious warmth of the propane heater and whirled to face her younger brother. Graydon might have dragged them out of the collapsed shelter, but he was still a pain in her ass.

He stood a couple of feet away, holding out a fresh pair of gloves.

"Me and Luke *nothing*." She jammed her numb hands into the dry fleece and glared at him.

He lifted his eyebrows. "Pretty cozy-looking *nothing*."

"We were stuck! He'd yanked me toward the entrance—"

"Never mind," her brother said. "Thought I saw something."

"Only me being angry with him," she insisted. Luke's absurd comments about her relationship habits surfaced from under the shock of the shelter collapse. How dare he imply she threw around *I love you*s like candy?

Love didn't show up just anywhere. And Emma could pick out if a couple was going to make it from a mile away.

Usually.

Her own romances hadn't exactly panned out. Not for lack of trying, but too often her long-term boyfriends didn't quite measure up. Asking her to cancel on Sunday dinner with her family so they could catch a movie, or the one particular gem who'd been shocked she wasn't excited to do her future husband's ironing. More nebulous reasons, too—a gut feeling there was no spark, a lack of that standing-in-the-sunshine feeling she'd described to Luke. She wasn't giving up hope, though. One day she'd find someone equally wonderful to the partner Grammy had found in Gramps, someone who made her smile the way her ultra-practical mom did when her dad cracked jokes or sneaked up and kissed her in the barn.

And in the meantime, she'd purchase the lodge, restore it to its past glory—beyond it, in fact—and plan perfect days for people who'd found their forever love. Her heart panged for Luke and his unwillingness to find that for himself.

Her brother started giving her the EMT once-over. He dug a penlight out of the lodge's first aid kit and flicked it in front of her eyes.

She swatted at him. "Stop it. I'm fine."

"Checking for signs of concussion."

"I didn't hit my head."

You sure about that? Could explain why the tight, protective band of Luke's arms felt like freaking heaven.

"You scared me, screaming like you did." Gray's blue gaze darkened. "I was parking my truck. Thought someone was in real trouble. And when I saw it was you…"

She squeezed her eyes shut. "I screwed up. The whole point of helping today was to help Luke, and instead, I messed up." Crap. Would her mistake mean he wouldn't accept her help for the rest of the festival?

"How?"

"The shelter collapsed because of me."

"But Luke said—"

"He lied." She grimaced. Him covering up the truth made no sense.

Graydon's face crinkled with suspicion again.

"Stop it."

The crowd was busy at least, getting ready to build shelters of their own. Luke had used their failure as a cautionary tale, earned some laughs over it. Everyone seemed eager to get to it.

She rubbed her hands together and took a step back from her brother. He had a mother-hen streak a mile wide. "You've fussed over me enough. Go build your fort."

He grinned. "It's my year. Rafe and I have a plan to bring Aleja and Nora down."

"Oh, really? Teaming up with the enemy?" Emma wasn't being serious—unlike their older sister, Nora, she didn't have a problem with Rafe, who owned the ranch next to the Halloran spread. But Nora couldn't stand the man, so would no doubt be desperate to beat Rafe as she'd always tried to do in everything from high school 4-H to the recent county ranching organization leadership race. Nora pairing up with Aleja, her best friend who happened to be a local contractor and Rafe's sister to boot, made total sense.

She had no idea why Graydon had skin in the game, but she didn't feel like dedicating the brain-power to figure it out.

Today didn't have to be a total loss. She could salvage something out of the event.

Best not to waste a minute.

She threw herself into the event, ferrying hot drinks to the competitors and egging on rivalries.

"Nora, Aleja," she whispered to her sister and her friend as she passed by. "I think Rafe and Gray are copying your design. You might want to check on them."

Nora poked her beanie-clad head out from the shelter, where the two women had dug out enough snow for both of them to fit. Her eyes locked on Rafe, who was shoveling out a doorway identical to hers. "Those turkeys!"

"Ours'll be better, Nora," Aleja said from inside the small dugout. "We'll beat them."

"Hopefully you do better than I did." Emma smiled, wishing she had her own best friend here as a cheerleader. Maggie was in the Caribbean for two weeks with her husband, stepdaughter and the rest of the Reid crew. And Emma wasn't going to interrupt Maggie's first hot holiday with her new family to ask for advice about Luke.

Wishing her sister luck, Emma walked toward the neighboring shelter. Luke was only a few feet away, talking to a group of guests. He glanced over his shoulder at her, brows raised.

A tingling, uncomfortable sense of déjà vu washed over her. Weird. She'd never shared a moment like this with Luke, with the winter sun picking out bits of gold in his light brown hair and beard, his smile curious and knowing all at the same time. He turned back to his conversation. She still couldn't shake the odd familiarity.

Wait though… She *had* stared at the back of his head for an entire semester of high school. Sat at her desk trying to focus on novel studies and synthesis essays and dreading every time he turned around.

God, he'd even invited her out fishing once.

No, first he'd made fun of her for never having fished before.

"How is that possible? You're not grossed out by scales and guts, are you?" he'd teased, rotating in his desk so his T-shirt hugged his flat abs. He brushed a hand down his pecs and smiled. She knew he worked out a ton to earn those muscles, but did he have to be so obnoxious about showing them off?

"I live on a ranch. Nothing grosses me out," she'd said, emphasizing the last few words with air quotes.

Between making honor roll, playing volleyball and working for her parents, she'd had zero time to while away on something mind-numbing like fly fishing.

He'd lowered his voice. "Skip math with me this afternoon. I'll show you the best place to snag a beauty trout."

She'd let herself contemplate it for a second. The fishing would suck, but getting the chance to gut a fish and prove Luke wrong might be rewarding. Especially if they took a few minutes to laze on the riverbank. He might even take off his shirt…

Uh, Emma? You cannot skip school.

Right. That wasn't her role. Bea broke all the rules, Nora got the grades, Jack got the athletic trophies and Emma did everything in her power to try to find something for herself. The only notable thing she'd managed recently was to have her heart broken when her boyfriend dumped her on his way out of town to play college football last year.

As if Luke wasn't going to take off in similar fashion the second they slapped his diploma in his hand.

And as if she'd be able to explain any of that to him. "Have you not read the perfect attendance plaque, like, ever?"

"Uh, why would I?"

"I guess you wouldn't have a reason, with all the school you miss for hockey," she'd said. "My name's been on it three years running, and I'm not breaking my streak."

"Your loss. Though it'd be hard to keep steady standing in a river with your nose so high in the air."

"Are you calling me snobby?"

Shrugging, he'd flashed her one of his trademark *my teeth look good, but my biceps are even better* grins. The one he wore when he was out on the ice and wanted to flirt with a girl in the stands.

Ugh. How did girls fall for something so blatantly obvious?

Because it's hot.

And he was hotter in his thirties, especially in snow gear with those strong arms that had yanked her to safety.

Emma made a noise of protest. It was easier to be irritated with his younger self. *Nose so high in the air.* He'd been a jerk.

He'd also had a point.

He turned now, taller and broader with an edge of maturity that caught her right in all her needy parts. "Need something, Emma?"

She felt the blood drain from her face. "No. Of course not."

"And you're staring because…"

She stiffened. "Because, uh—I realized we forgot to put on music! I'll go hook it up."

Hurrying over to the event tent, she breathed deeply, trying to untwist her stomach. She set up a playlist of lively holiday music and cranked it loud.

Called out some encouragement on the microphone for good measure, earning a bemused smile from Luke.

He didn't look annoyed anymore. Maybe now, while everyone was busy, she could drop a few hints about her wedding lodge ideas.

A familiar-sounding cough rang out behind her.

She whirled to face the culprit. "Hank Emerson, you should be in bed." She waved him over to a chair.

He sat with a rough sigh. "My doctor wants me to move a little every day, and I'm not going to pass this to anyone. Thought I'd enjoy the sunshine for a spell."

"Luke and I have everything under control," she assured him.

"Damn right." Luke stalked around the drinks table and entered the tent. "What are you doing over here, Grandpa? Could you be more mule-headed?"

As if Luke could point fingers—he'd inherited that particular demeanor.

Was imitating it right now, in fact.

A chuckle escaped Emma's throat.

"See, son? Nothing better than some festive music, fresh air and the laugh of a beautiful woman."

"Rascal." Emma nudged Hank's shoulder with a gentle elbow.

"Good thing you have her help today," he said to Luke. "You'd be overwhelmed without her expertise."

"Expertise?" Luke drew back. "She almost got us smothered in our shelter."

Hank looked puzzled. "Smothered?"

"Oh, sure, now you throw me under the bus," she muttered.

"Nothing, Grandpa." Luke pulled his cell from his pocket and scanned the screen. His forehead wrinkled. "Excuse me for a second."

He greeted the caller and walked a few yards away, expression darkening by the second.

Emma kept one eye on him and one on Hank, chatting with the older man as he admired the decorated trees from a distance.

"Your rainbow entry sure sticks out, Emma," he said.

She smiled. "The girls insisted on all the colors."

Luke, on the other hand, was downright frowning as he said goodbye to whomever was on the other line. He palmed the top of his knit hat and closed his eyes, jamming the device in his pocket.

"Problem?" she called over to him.

He rejoined them. "Uh, yeah. The dance school that's supposed to perform on day nine and run classes on day ten is having to cancel due to illness. Bad flu bug running through the place. We're down not one, but two events."

Emma winced in concert with Hank's groan.

"Don't worry about it, Grandpa. I'll figure something out," Luke said, words far more confident than his tone.

"Nine ladies dancing?" Emma asked, racking her brain for ideas.

"Yep," Luke said.

Dancing... Christmas... "The Nutcracker." She

held up a finger. "Not as a performance. One of the movie versions. Hold a family movie night in the lodge."

Hank's face lit up. "Great idea, darlin'. Easy to arrange on short notice."

Luke scrunched his face in reluctant acceptance. "Good call, Em."

"I'm sure I could think of something for 'ten lords a-leaping,' too," she said.

"Grandpa and I will come up with a replacement," Luke said.

"Oh, I don't know, son. I like seeing Emma take charge. Reminds me of your grandmother. You're skilled in the forest and the river, but event planning is out of your wheelhouse."

"Grandpa..." Hurt edged Luke's low tone.

Her stomach ached at the flicker of vulnerability.

"Luke knows what he's doing, Hank. He loves this festival, and it makes sense for him to be in charge," she said. "But he's shorthanded. I can keep pitching in, if you like. It'd be my pleasure."

Pleasure? Luke mouthed over Hank's head.

She couldn't even glare back, not with Hank looking at her like she'd hung the moon.

"I feel like it's too much to expect at this time of year," Hank said.

"I don't mind. It's been fun so far." She didn't look at Luke, lest he mouth *fun?* at her in an equally infuriating way. "I don't want you to feel like you owe me. All I ask is for you to consider my purchase offer before you officially put the place on the market."

Luke choked on his hot chocolate.

Hank nodded. "Completely fair."

"Fair?" Luke snapped.

Completely, Emma emphasized silently.

"Real mature, Halloran."

"Oh, we're last-naming each other now?" She supposed it was his comfort zone, having been a team-sport athlete for so long.

He looked up at the tent ceiling in clear frustration. "You need my approval, too, *Emma*."

Did he mean the emphasis to be snide? In his deep, rumbling, rich bourbon voice, it came off as a caress. Heat licked her cheeks.

Her belly, too.

Argh, she was getting distracted. "Why do I need your approval? Do you own part of the property?"

"No, but Grandpa agreed he wouldn't put the place on the market without consulting Brody and me."

He had? Hmm. "Okay, that'll be part of the deal," she said. "I help—"

Luke opened his mouth to protest.

She held up a hand. "You know you need it."

He lifted a shoulder.

She needed more than a shrug—without his promise to listen, she couldn't be sure they had an agreement.

"I help," she repeated, "and you take me seriously."

Her pulse thrummed as she waited for his reply.

He didn't seem in a hurry to give it. With his sharp glare and his thermal shirt hugging his pecs under his unzipped jacket, he looked angry and delicious and like he held her future in his hands.

Crap, there was nothing good about any of that.

Luke poured two hot chocolates, stuck a candy cane in one and handed it to his grandpa. He paused, looking at her. "Want one?"

"Not if it's that much effort."

"Of course it isn't." Luke shoved a filled paper cup into her hands.

She was torn between being infuriated at his delayed answer and smiling because he'd plunked a candy cane in her drink. "Do you agree, Luke?"

"No." A long breath gusted from his lips. "Before I agree to you helping, you have to be honest with Grandpa about everything," he said. "The shift to weddings *and* scrapping the festival."

Chapter Four

Hank sat against his chair and blinked at Emma. The sadness in his eyes almost cut her off at the knees. "That true, Emma? You'd cancel the festival?"

Her heart leaped into her throat. "Not exactly. Like I told Luke earlier, I can't say I'd run a snow fort competition, or be able to do a twelve-day-long event." She sent the snitch in question an icy look. "You know I'd make the holidays a thousand percent special. What's more romantic than Christmas?"

"That was my grandma's opinion, too. Hence starting this tradition." Luke downed his drink and crumpled the empty cup in his fist.

The song on the speakers switched to "Winter Wonderland."

Ha. Not quite. Not with Luke poking holes in her vision.

She held his flashing gaze. "This place is about my grandmother, too."

"Not for over thirty years," he said sharply.

"True. But history is relevant," she murmured. "And her favorite part of running the resort was weddings. I want to build on that."

"The lodge isn't a destination for bridezillas to litter with fussy flowerpots and hand-painted signs and Great Dane–shaped cookies."

He was describing her best friend Maggie's wedding, the gorgeous one held last summer. Emma had helped plan it down to the final detail.

Hank's gaze shifted between them. "Luke."

She put a hand on the older man's shoulder and squeezed, a silent *I got this*. "Don't you dare insult one of the best days of my friend's life."

He said nothing, though his scowl suggested he knew he'd totally crossed a line.

Find someone who can admit he's in the wrong, Emma. Her grandmother's voice. Yeah, Luke would never live up to that gem of wisdom.

Her hands twitched, tempted to dump the giant carafe of cocoa over his head.

"And the rest, Emma?" Luke was clearly still on the attack. "You're going to make sure your guests are here for outdoor sports? Keep the partnership going with the rod and gun club?"

"Well, no," she admitted.

"You'd cut out the entire purpose of the place."

"What do I need to do to show you I'm serious about this?" she asked Luke.

"I know you're serious," he said. "But your plan is flawed."

"Your grandpa's willing to listen," she said.

"Is this why you've stayed buddy-buddy with him? Ingratiating yourself to get the lodge?"

Hot anger ripped along her limbs. "Absolutely not."

"You're way out of line, Luke," Hank said in a low voice. "Emma's been nothing but lovely to me since Ted and Winnie's accident, making sure I let myself grieve and don't get too lonely. She and I have talked many a time about different futures for the lodge."

"You're clueless about the value of this place." Luke stared at her. His eyes flashed. Not with temper. With…loss.

Her heart squeezed. His delivery had been ugly, and she wanted to hold on to her fury, but the near anguish in his eyes was like splashing a bucket of water on a campfire. He saw her as a threat. She needed to change that. And she couldn't blame him for protecting Hank or for caring so deeply about a business that had been in his family since he was a preschooler. "If I'm clueless, then show me why it's special to you. During the festival. If you're willing to listen to my reasons for wanting the place, it's only fair I return the gesture."

Hank cleared his throat. "You listening is non-negotiable, Luke. Her business plan deserves your honest appraisal."

Luke stared into the distance for a few long seconds, looking down the berm at the competitors, not seeming to really see them. Lord, his size and strength were even more obvious when he took that hands-on-hips position innate to law enforcement officers. And he might spend a lot of his day counting animals and dealing with roadkill and boat licenses, but every few weeks, the local paper featured something about him facing down a cranky hunter or a person ill-trained to use firearms.

Something panged low in her belly.

Hunger, probably. She *had* missed lunch.

When he finally looked back at Hank, his face was blank. "Okay, Grandpa. I'll listen. Promise."

Rising to his feet, Hank nodded. "Good. I'll be able to rest easier knowing the festival's in experiènced hands."

Luke's cheek flinched.

Oof. Being underestimated was the worst. How many times had Emma felt like that in her own family?

His gaze landed on her. A searchlight, almost catching the things she hid in the shadows.

Pressing her lips together, she stared into her hot chocolate. She wasn't going to let him see those soft parts, scraped raw from knowing the people who loved her didn't truly understand her.

She wasn't going to contribute to his own self-doubt, either. Lifting her chin, she connected with his steely gray gaze. "We'll do it together."

Early the next evening, Luke gripped the steering wheel of his truck, cursing the report he'd just received. There was an injured elk on one of Sutter Creek's backroads—not something that could wait for tomorrow.

He groaned at the prospect of another long night. He'd had a crap sleep, tossing and turning. By the time the sun had peeked through the blinds, he'd been as stiff as if he'd been wrestling a grizzly instead of sweaty sheets.

He'd take a bear over grappling with the harebrained scheme of one Emma Halloran.

No doubt she'd be thrilled his work call meant she'd get to take over preparations for the third day of Christmas—an intimate three-course chicken dinner following his grandma's recipes. Not exactly a French hen, though it always brought in a crowd.

"Silent Night" came on the radio, as if the DJ was taunting him. Between the extra hours and having to get along with Emma for his grandfather's sake, tonight would be anything but silent. He turned off the song and dialed her number.

They'd been going back and forth over text all day, but him missing dinner required an actual call.

"Hello, Lucas," she greeted.

"That's not my name."

She snickered. "Hello, Luke Henry Franklin Emerson."

"Wait, you know my middle names?"

She paused. "We talked about it in class once."

"A long time ago," he said. "Sorry, I can't remember yours."

"Winifred," she said quietly. "After Grammy."

"Of course." Her confession yesterday about the lodge's connection to her grandmother was eating at him. He'd been so focused on hating what she wanted to do to the place, he hadn't considered *why* she was so hell-bent on it. Winnie Dawson had given endless amounts of time and love to her family and community over her lifetime, and Emma's desire to emulate and honor her made sense.

She'd have to find a different way to do it. He'd promised he'd tolerate her involvement for the festival, but the second the final event wrapped up, he'd thank her politely and send her on her way.

Tonight, though, he could admit—reluctantly—he was fortunate to have her to fill in. "Bad news, Em. I got a call about an injured elk a few minutes ago."

"Oh, no!"

"I know. It's crap timing."

"Luke," she said. "Don't worry about the timing. The poor animal… Go find it, okay? You can pitch in whenever you're done. I have things under control."

Pitch in. At his grandfather's business.

"Thank you, Emma. I appreciate it."

Silence.

"Did I lose you?" he asked.

"No, uh…" She cleared her throat. "Be safe, Luke."

"Always am."

At 10:00 p.m., he pulled into the parking lot, bone tired and ready to sack out in his cabin. Her car was still there. His grandfather's living room and bedroom lights were off, so she wasn't visiting Hank. Was she still in the main building?

So much for a hot shower and cool sheets.

He flipped up the collar of his work coat against the wind and made his way into the building, nodding at the night front desk clerk and striding down the long hallway to the dining room. The overhead lights were off. Pleated glass wall sconces lit the large room with a gentle glow, glinting off the silver tinsel garland lining the balcony of the loft above the kitchen. The Christmas decorations centering each of the tables seemed to have tripled in size.

Sparkly swags lined the windows overlooking the Moosehorn River, too. Had they been there the last time he looked? And what the hell was going on over the mantel of the river-rock fireplace? A Santa-and-reindeer wall hanging graced the place of honor instead of the stuffed fish that had decorated the stone for decades.

His fish.

Emma. That's what was going on.

"Halloran? You here?"

"In the nook," she called out.

He shuffled past the mix of round and long rectangular tables. The scent of richly sauced chicken and stuffing still hung in the air. His mouth watered.

Faint music played from the built-in speakers, an acoustic guitar rendition of "The Christmas Waltz." The slow melody of his favorite holiday song brought his pulse down a notch or two.

He rounded the corner into the small sunroom. The

most well-loved—and most comfortable—furniture on the property had the honor of filling the space. A three-seater, eye-strain-inducing flowered couch, and two jewel-blue velvet chairs worn in all the right places. His grandmother's antique German Christmas spinning pyramid, its four circular tiers themed with tiny figures of the Twelve Days of Christmas, sat motionless in a place of honor under the window.

As a kid, he'd begged his grandmother to light the candles the minute her annual order arrived from Germany. He'd sat on the floor enrapt, watching the propellor at the top spin from the heat of the flames, turning the tiers and making the silly geese taunt the maids a-milking and the ladies dance with the lords.

Smiling at the reminder of the small things that made Christmas special, he nodded at Emma.

She was curled up on one corner of the couch. Tiny snowmen danced on her leggings, and a cozy-looking navy sweater hugged her frame, the edge kissing her thighs. She pushed up her glasses and studied him. The green of her eyes tugged at him, prodded the sensitive parts a hard night on the job scraped open. He hated having to put an animal down.

He slung himself into one of the chairs, adjusting his utility belt when it dug into his hips. "I take it you've been decorating, honey?"

Honey? Where on earth had that come from? Damn, he was tired.

He rested his head on the back of the chair and sighed. He didn't have it in him to spar with her tonight, couldn't even brace himself for whatever snarky advance she'd been preparing all night.

Nothing came. She just watched him with those luminous eyes, taking him apart a few pieces at a time with every beat of silence.

"Where's my fish?" he said.

"Safely packed away for the holidays," she said cautiously. "People don't want a trout staring at them while they're enjoying a romantic dinner."

"My grandfather and I caught that fish when I was five. It's almost thirty years old," he growled.

"I could tell." Her usual sarcasm was gentled.

"I want my fish back."

She pulled the corner of her lower lip into her mouth and worried the plush, pink flesh. "You've had two late nights this week."

"I have two late nights a lot of weeks," he said. "Or more. It's not a job you go into because the hours are good."

"You love it, though."

He nodded.

"And the elk?"

He scrubbed a hand down his face. "Somewhere out there, a vehicle has a hell of a crunched-up front end."

She winced. "Poor animal."

"Yep. Sorry I missed dinner."

"It's okay. I can—"

"Handle it. I know." He curved up one side of his mouth, needing not to feel sad. To erase her serious expression, too. "And me, apparently."

Her cheeks pinkened.

I can handle the cold. And you. He'd laughed when she'd made that claim the night of the tree unveiling. There were way too many ways to take that statement. The way it was intended—she was an overachiever who refused to let go of something once she sank her teeth into it.

Or the way it had him thinking of her pretty hands handling his body.

Except she seemed more intent to use those pretty hands to mess with his grandfather's legacy.

He understood the place had meaning to her family, too, but it was more important to the Emersons. More important to *Luke*. He had failed to build on Hank's glory as a hockey player. Damn if he'd let his grandpa's reputation as a conservationist disappear, too.

"Have you even thought of the impact on fish and wildlife in the area if the lodge becomes a haven for people with no regard for the environment?" he asked.

"Better than having the property rezoned as residential," she said between gritted teeth.

"That won't happen. If he's insistent on retiring, I'm going to make sure a buyer continues with our current business model."

"You can't control that, Luke."

"I disagree."

"So you lied to him when you promised Hank you'd listen to what I had to say?"

It was his turn to growl. "*Listen* and *change my mind* are not synonyms."

"Thanks for the English lesson. Ms. Rogers would be so proud." She examined her nails, one of those hours-long salon jobs, no doubt. Pale gold with bits of red and white.

A manicure like that would last three seconds in the wild. Back when he was a foolish kid, he'd actually believed Emma would be interested in coming out on the river with him. Had asked her to skip class to do it. It had been in English class, come to think of it. But while he'd been good at learning language definitions and poetic devices—Ms. Rogers had been one of a handful of teachers who'd known how to help him navigate his dyslexia—he'd been crap at figuring out Emma.

She was still throwing him for a loop.

"I don't break promises to my grandpa," he grumbled.

"Good."

"Didn't say I'd make it easy on you, though."

"No big deal," she said. "I like hard."

He coughed. "Do you now?"

"Not like that!"

"Sure, firecracker."

Her pupils widened, leaving only a hint of green. "Not like that…with you."

Ouch. "You could have headed home after cleanup."

"You and I need to debrief every day." Tossing her book on the table, she pointed toward the kitchen. "I made you a plate. It's in the fridge."

"You're serious? That's—" His stomach growled. "Necessary?"

He chuckled. "I'll go heat it up."

When he got back to the nook with his food, Emma was talking to someone on the phone.

Your grandfather, she mouthed.

Sitting on the opposite end of the couch from her, he shoveled a bite of savory chicken and stuffing into his mouth and groaned as the flavors hit his taste buds. Heaven. No stuffing recipe ever lived up to Jenny Emerson's.

"You should have waited until the morning to call," Emma said into the sleek device. "Of course, everything went fine with dinner. Luke's with me now. I'll put you on speakerphone."

Emma tapped the screen and set the device on the cushion between them.

"Dinner's more than fine. I can't believe I missed this meal for work," Luke said. "Didn't think you'd be up, Grandpa."

"Could say the same about you both. Poor Emma's yawned five times in the last two minutes."

She looked at Luke and shook her head. "I'm fine, Hank."

"Nonsense. Look, I've been thinking. One of the reasons I've been able to manage this festival in the past years is because I live on the property. Emma, darlin', Luke's already staying in one of the double cabins. I think you should take the half adjoining his."

Her "Hank—" and his "Oh, no, I don't—" rang out in stereo.

"None of that. It's only day three, and you're both dead on your feet. I can hear it in your voices. Emma, what is this for you, hour fourteen?"

"Yes," she admitted.

He harrumphed. "You working here is allowing me to recuperate, but I won't be able to if I'm having to worry about you getting run off your feet and driving home in the middle of the night. The room is decent enough, and it'll be a place to rest your head."

Emma's mouth twisted. "What about Splotches? I don't think she'd like being alone in a cabin all day."

Luke shot her a questioning look.

"My cat."

He nodded. Envy twinged in his chest. He'd love to have a pet, a dog, especially, but his hours didn't allow it.

"Splotches can stay with me," Hank said. "Company during my convalescence." He coughed. It almost sounded purposeful.

"Bea's going to be visiting, staying with my parents," Emma protested.

"And you'll be closer to the ranch if you stay here than if you were in town."

Emma, asleep in a room next to him… He could fight off the image of her sleek body entwined in the lodge's striped sheets if it meant keeping Grandpa on his couch.

Luke forked in more dinner. "He's not going to give in," he murmured around the bite.

"Fine. I'll bring a suitcase with me tomorrow."

"Knew you had some sense in you." Hank's voice brimmed with victory.

Victorious over what?

Luke narrowed his eyes at the phone. The coughing, pushing them to work together, insisting on the adjacent rooms—holy hell, was Hank trying his hand at being Cupid?

"Wrong holiday, Grandpa," he said under his breath.

Emma said goodbye and disconnected the call. "What did you say?"

"My grandfather." He laughed. "I think he's playing matchmaker."

Incredulity spread on Emma's face. Her lips split into a grin, followed by a laugh, long and hearty and soul-warming. It took her a full thirty seconds to calm down enough to say, "Oh, that's rich."

"You and I both know he can try all he wants—he won't succeed."

Her smile faltered for a second. "Of course not. He's dreaming if he thinks I'm going to fall head over heels for you while you do wildlife calls tomorrow."

Luke crossed his arms. "You think I can't make mating calls sexy, honey?"

She scoffed. "No one can."

"Bet I could."

"Twenty bucks says it's impossible. But I'd like to see you try."

Chapter Five

"Oh, my God. If I was a moose, I'd totally jump him."

"Bea!" Emma flicked the white bobble on her sister's Santa hat. "You're almost engaged. God. Control yourself."

Bea tucked her short, platinum blond curls behind her ears and readjusted the sparkly red cap. "Around that show of manly confidence? Why?"

"Because he's making *moose* noises." With an exaggerated shudder, Emma did a quick check to make sure no one in the crowd filling the lodge's dining hall was paying attention to them. There were a good hundred people milling about. For the four-dollar red-and-green drinks, no doubt. The attempts at sounding like wildlife were an entertaining bonus, and were getting more outlandish as the night went on. Good thing Hank had hired a bus to shuttle people back into town.

"The grunts are ridiculous, sure." Bea sipped her lurid emerald drink through a straw. "But Luke's commitment is sexy."

It was.

He was MC-ing the animal call competition with ease, throwing in his expertise on occasion, generally looking like a red-flannel-shirt-covered snack. He had on a Santa hat, too, plush and green. Emma had expected a protest when she'd plucked it out of her festive bag of tricks as they were setting up, but he'd donned it with no fuss.

He turned to say something to the next person up to the microphone.

Emma wobbled on her stiletto ankle boots.

From them being high, obviously. Not from realizing Luke still had a hockey butt.

"Wow," Bea breathed the word.

"I know." Emma said on a moan. "Those jeans make his ass look like it was blessed by God."

More accurately, anyone who appreciates a man's rear view is blessed to be in the presence of Luke's.

"Are you checking out my cousin?"

Brody Emerson's laugh made it clear the question wasn't serious.

"No!" Emma shook her head hard enough she almost lost her elf-hat fascinator headband.

Bea rolled her eyes and tossed back the rest of her drink.

A grin gracing his handsome face, Brody nudged his lean athlete's body between the sisters. He clinked his longneck against Emma's low-ball glass.

"Whole lot of doth-protesting going on there, Em," Brody teased.

She elbowed him in the gut. "I'll show you 'doth-protesting.'"

Brody groaned. "Some Christmas welcome."

He'd arrived from Seattle this morning on the same flight as Emma's sister. Bea had never been afflicted by her sisters' inability to make friends with their neighbors—she and Brody had always been besties.

Emma understood the ease of their friendship. Brody was mellow, lacking his older cousin's stubborn, cocksure nature. Life seemed to come easy to the world-class rower, now coach. A good foil for Bea, who never failed to complicate her life with her big dreams and lack of focus.

How she'd ended up seriously dating an investment banker instead of someone more like Brody, Emma didn't know.

But Emma had her own Emerson to worry about.

Stop right there, Luke is not my Emerson.

Brody started whispering in Bea's ear about something, and Emma tuned them out, scanning the room to see if anything needed attending to.

Her eyes landed on Luke.

Yeah, no. *He* did not need "attending to."

She took a long sip of her gingerbread-whiskey cocktail, trying to savor the one alcoholic drink she'd let herself have. She and Luke had figured they would be more useful as the social faces of the evening.

Putting his own drink on the podium next to the fireplace, he shook out his hands. With a gentle breath, he twittered into the microphone, the playful sound a million times prettier than the guttural grunt of a big game animal. His eyes drifted shut. Big roughened hands cupped around his mouth, fingers fluttering in a rapid, practiced rhythm.

A rhythm that would feel perfect between her thighs…

Heat pooled beneath her mistletoe-print panties. "Son of a bitch, I owe him twenty dollars."

Luke's gaze, intense and focused, connected with hers from across the room.

Another hot wave rushed through her.

She spun around, breaking the connection.

Bea and Brody looked at her like she'd lost her mind.

Panic blitzed through her stomach. "I need to check on something in the kitchen."

She needed *air*.

She left her half-full drink on a bistro table and escaped through the double doors connecting the dining room and the food prep area. The long employees-only hallway, lined with notice boards and framed, decades-old lodge advertisements, led to the far end of the overhang-covered porch. She escaped out the door.

Cold smacked her in the face. She inhaled, welcoming the chill on her too-warm skin. A minute or two, and she'd find her center again.

Find a way to stop feeling turned on around Luke, you mean.

The decorated trees twinkled around her, a row of glittering sentries against the log-sided wall. A few couples and families wandered under the overhang, chatting and smiling, examining the creations.

No one appeared to notice Emma.

Not good enough—she wanted to be alone. Somewhere free from the reminder of Luke being adorable with her Brownies or protective as he sheltered her from the collapsing snow cave.

Somewhere free of her grandmother's mischievous advice—*make sure your man is passionate about what matters to him, including you.*

"Really would love having you here for in-person advice, Grammy. Between Luke and the lodge, I could use it," she whispered into the dark.

Spinning on the heel of her boot, she untangled her pashmina from her neck and wrapped it around her shoulders. Not the best choice in twenty-eight-degree weather, but she wouldn't literally freeze. The light walk looked blessedly empty. She headed toward the multicolored archway marking the start of the path through the forest, spiky boot heels sinking into the snow with each step.

Each gleaming bulb unwound the knot in her stomach a bit more. Hanging balls of lights and pale-blue-light-wrapped trunks created a magical, glowing wonderland.

Oh, wow… This path would be amazing for wedding photography. And for guests. She'd have to point out to Luke that there were some parts of Emerson tradition she could carry forward.

Better. Be calm. Be in control. This will be worth it.

Boot steps crunched in the snow at the entrance to the path behind her.

A heavy, familiar, confident stride.

Her heart sank. She'd wanted to finish the half-mile stroll in peace.

He approached her with worried eyes, shucking out of his winter work jacket.

He didn't stop walking until he was less than two feet from her, close enough to drape the garment over her shoulders. The weight landed on her like an embrace. His outdoor-spice scent swamped her.

She'd been working *so* hard to ignore that deliciousness, and now—

He tucked her hair behind her ear with a warm, rough fingertip. "It's not safe to be out here alone at night."

Safer than being out here with you.

"I'm fine. Wasn't going to go far."

"You could have come across an animal."

For once, it didn't feel like he was lecturing her. Something beyond professional concern darkened his eyes. Something like *caring*.

She stiffened. "We're surrounded by Christmas lights and people smells. I don't think any wily bobcat is going to come looking for their next meal."

"You don't know that." His mouth twitched. "They might think it's a glitzy bobcat buffet."

A grin pulled at her lips, no matter how much she didn't want to reward him for his cheesy joke.

He didn't grin back. Pupils blown wide, he stared at her mouth.

From the dim light, surely. It couldn't have anything to do with her.

He cupped her cheek. "Emma…"

Oh. Maybe a little to do with her.

And those fingers, softly tracing her jaw—

She took a deep breath. "I owe you that twenty."

The satisfaction she would have expected to see on his face never materialized. He bent his head to hers, lips brushing her temple.

A hint of a touch.

One she could pretend hadn't happened, if she wanted to.

She didn't.

"I thought you looked impressed." His breath warmed her ear. His mouth, too, nuzzling her cheek.

A thumb, stroking the corner of her lips.

Her knees weakened. She slid her palms up his muscled chest. Not for separation. For something to cling to. A weight settled at the base of her spine. His other hand. It pulled her in, the heat of her belly pressing against his hardness.

A gasp filled the forest.

Hers.

Inside the cocoon of his jacket and his sexy scent,

with his flannel shirt warming her fingers, it was impossible to care about the needy admission.

His lips murmured something about sweet lemons against her cheek. That mouth… Why the hell wasn't it on hers yet?

Splaying a hand, she ran her palm along his beard. Softer than she expected, smelling of some warm, woodsy fragrance.

A nudge, and he claimed her lips.

Holy God, Luke Emerson could kiss.

Tender, purposeful, like all he wanted to do was overwhelm every ounce of her awareness, pulling her into a momentary heaven. A blur of seconds, of minutes, where only his kiss, his hands, existed. And the pleasure she could find there.

Her head spun. He tasted like honesty. Like promises and openness and all the certainty she wanted from life.

All the things she knew he had no interest in giving to a woman.

Tearing her lips away, she scrambled backward. Her boot heels dug into the snow and she pitched backward. Her butt landed hard on the packed ground and she yelped. Momentum carried her farther, and her head hit the trail with sharp reverberation. Cold seeped through her hair.

Luke was beside her in a fraction of a second, swearing and gathering her up, settling her on his knees. "I thought… I'm sorry. One word, and I would have stopped."

She squeezed her eyes shut, rubbing the back of her smarting skull. "I didn't want you to stop."

He tilted her chin with a finger. To kiss her again?

No, to examine her face. His other hand gently tested the spot where her head had hit the ground.

"So next time, save yourself the pain and keep kissing me," he said.

"Next time? That's not your style, Luke. You're not a forever guy."

She'd take a headache over heartache any time.

She climbed off his lap as gracefully as possible, dropping his jacket in the space she'd vacated.

It was freezing without the layer of protection, but wearing the garment made her more vulnerable than the weather ever could.

He rose from the ground, gaze unwavering.

She spun and headed to the lodge. Away from Luke and his too-good mouth, from not-promises and not-forever.

Toward the goals she could control. Plans that would never let her down.

Thwack. Crack.
Thwack. Crack.

Luke jammed his spare pillow over his head, trying to muffle the noise of some eager employee chopping wood at 8:00 a.m. on a Friday. His first morning of vacation, nine solid days of not freezing his ass off with the ongoing marsh cleanup or getting called into the woods, and he couldn't even sleep in.

Not that Christmas at Emerson Wilderness Lodge

normally involved sleeping in. Twelve Days of Free Grandson Labor Festival was more like it.

Luke would happily keep sacrificing his time. Even if his grandfather thought it wasn't "in his wheelhouse." The lodge was about everything Grandpa had built after his illustrious hockey career. Hockey players from Hank's era hadn't made what they did now, so he'd needed to work, first as the Dawsons' maintenance manager and then buying the place from them.

The property had been Luke's safe space growing up. Still was, really. He loved every inch of it—the trails he'd cut with his grandpa, and watching Hank teach people to love and respect the river where he'd first shown Luke how to cast a line.

How could Hank be talking about letting that go? Didn't it mean as much to him as it did to Luke?

Brody living in Washington complicated things, as did Hank's claim that Luke would be miserable giving up his game warden position to take charge. His throat tightened. There had to be a way to keep it in the family.

The wood chopper hadn't slowed down at all, and between the sharp cracks and his whirling mind, Luke was fully awake.

Groaning, he rolled onto his back and slung his arm over his eyes. No way was he rushing to get up. Between tomorrow's 6K Snowshoe Goose Chase and Sunday's Swans-a-Swimming River Plunge, he'd be up before the sun all weekend.

Tonight was couples' trivia night and carried the

most coveted prize of the festival, a gold ring donated by a local jeweler. It'd be another late night, and he was starting to see his grandpa's point about Emma staying on property.

Though why she needed to be close enough to share a wall with Luke, he wasn't sure.

Scratch that, he was sure—Hank had hearts in his eyes and was projecting them onto Luke and Emma.

Going off how she'd bolted after their kiss in the light walk last night, those matchmaking efforts were a waste of time. The kiss hadn't been the problem. Incredible, more like it.

You're not a forever guy.

Never had been, not even with the people who were supposed to love him most.

His dad hadn't bothered to even know him. His mom, who'd had him at nineteen, had left Sutter Creek the second he finished high school. Married and had a kid with Luke's stepdad before Luke had finished his first year in the minors. And his fiancée had dumped his ass the minute his NHL team decided not to sign him. Hank and Brody were the only people who'd stuck by Luke, despite his humiliating crash and burn. He owed them for that.

And Emma had him one hundred percent pegged. It didn't matter how good she tasted, how right it felt to make her melt and moan in his arms. She didn't tolerate mistakes.

She'd clearly labeled their kiss as such.

Was she trying to sleep in, too? Lying in the bed that mirrored his, tangled in white sheets…

Focusing on her dark hair spilling across the pillows would be nothing but trouble.

He got up, showered, dressed and made himself coffee with the single-serving machine in the cabin's small kitchenette, all to the soundtrack of insistent wood-chopping.

Ceramic mug in hand, he made his way onto the covered, wood-planked porch.

He almost dropped the coffee.

A pink-cheeked Emma stood about twenty yards away, next to the equipment shed. A thick log topped a chopping block, bracketed by two heaping piles of wood. She'd stripped down to a long-sleeved T-shirt, black leggings and the Sorels she'd worn during the shelter competition. She gripped a maul in gloved hands. One swift motion, and she cleaved a thick log in two.

Luke's mouth dried out.

"Emma?" he croaked.

She didn't respond, centered one of the two newly split chunks and drove the maul into it.

Holy. Hell.

Two inches of fresh snow carpeted the ground. It sifted across his boots as he crossed the expanse. He circled around the front of the woodpiles in case she had her headphones in.

Another driving sweep. Another crack.

He swallowed an appreciative groan.

"Who put you on wood detail?" he said.

She held the ax shaft in both hands, horizontal across her hips. He hadn't gotten the chance to test those curves last night, not enough. He could guess at their softness, but without a long study—

"Luke?" She stared at him, gaze cool.

Worlds away from the heat in her eyes and her parted lips last night.

"Luke."

He jolted. "What?"

"You were staring."

Oof. Couldn't deny that. "Sorry."

"I was trying to tell you I was up early, so I volunteered for wood duty."

Wood duty? Did she not hear herself sometimes? Or maybe he was stuck in twelve-year-old boy mode.

But the sight of her splitting hunks of wood with the heavy ax... *Hey. Loser. Enough.*

Right. Fantasizing about her would get him nowhere. He'd be better off relying on the snark they'd been trading since childhood.

"Chop away. Though you might chip that manicure of yours," he said.

The dismissive words felt foreign on his tongue. *Asshole, much?*

Her glare was as sharp as the icicles hanging off the roof of the shed. "Don't you have some marmots to count somewhere?"

He deserved that, and more. He shook his head.

"Planning on ruining some fishers' days instead?"

He sighed. "When you choose not to follow regulations, you're asking—"

Her mouth twitched.

Ah. Yanking his chain, then.

"I'm not planning on ruining anyone's day. I'm on vacation now, remember? And the last eight days of the festival are some of the best. I need to drive into town to pick up tonight's prize from the jeweler. Do you need anything?"

The pompom on her knit hat waggled as she shook her head.

Another item from his to-do list popped into his head. He'd meant to talk to her about it yesterday after MC-ing the animal call competition. She'd never been one to make fun of his awkward reading aloud back in high school. Hopefully that hadn't changed.

"Could you do me a favor tonight?" he asked.

"Probably."

"Last night I realized there's no way I can MC the trivia competition. It's too much reading aloud on the spot." His brain loved to take in one word and spit out a different one. "Without time to focus, I'm bound to misread words and screw up the game. Can you take it on?"

Her wide smile lacked any of her earlier irritation. "Of course. Happy to."

"Great. I think we're all set."

"Oh, you came up with a tenth-day event?"

He shook his head. His stomach knotted. He hated not being able to come through for his grandfather with a brilliant idea. "Still working on it."

"Luke…" She chewed her lip.

He cocked his head, waiting for her to elaborate.

God knew he needed extra time to think sometimes. He wasn't going to rush her.

"Lords a-leaping," she mused. "Got me thinking about figure skating. And with the lake frozen early this year—what about holding a skating session?"

Skating. The knot in his belly drew tighter. "That's a lot of red tape, Emma. I don't see putting it together in time to advertise."

"You think I can't draw a crowd with short notice?" she said lightly. "Trust me, if you figure out the logistics, I can make sure everyone knows about it."

Something crumpled in his chest. A part of him he kept shoved deep, kept away from anything to do with the sport he'd loved and failed at. The "logistics" had nothing to do with waivers and ice safety. The complication would be stepping onto the ice where he'd carved up the smooth surface with his grandfather on the new skates he got for Christmas every year from the time he was four until the year he got rejected by his major-league team.

Hank hadn't bought Luke a pair since.

He'd never managed the courage to ask if his grandpa had broken the tradition to spare Luke's feelings or due to Hank's own disappointment.

He clenched his jaw. "It wouldn't be safe."

"People have been skating over by the public beach."

"It's not the same."

"Luke." Her tone softened. "What's the issue?"

He blurted out the first thing he could think of to distract her from the truth. "About last night…"

Her smile vanished. "Don't."

"But—"

"What's there to say? You looked cute in your Santa hat. We were alone and got carried away." Her shoulders straightened and her chin tilted. "People kiss all the time, Luke."

Not like that.

And she wouldn't be making weak excuses if it hadn't affected her.

Shooting her a forced-as-hell grin, he said, "I was just going to say it's forgotten."

Thankfully, she didn't call out his lie.

Chapter Six

Luke barely saw Emma the rest of the day. All the jobs she busied herself with were somewhere he wasn't, and he couldn't decide if he was happy about the space or not. Didn't matter that he hadn't seen her in person, though—he couldn't get the picture of her competently chopping wood out of his head. He was still envisioning it as the guests started arriving for the trivia event.

Emma was sorting through cue cards over by the coffee station, wearing a pair of shiny, tight red pants. Best removed like gift wrap: slowly, fully savoring the surprise beneath. And her shoes, spangled gold with a strap across her slender foot—those weren't Friday-night-at-a-wilderness-lodge shoes. They were girls'-weekend-in-Seattle shoes. New-Year's-in-Times-Square shoes.

Wrapped-around-me-digging-into-my-back shoes.

Gritting his teeth, he got back to work hanging the game board on the wall.

He had to stop letting dirty thoughts slide past his mental block. After the festival was over and he had dissuaded her from her wedding lodge scheme, they were still going to need to live in the same town and associate with the same people. Hell, tonight mattered, too. A bunch of their friends and family were in the audience, some even competing for the gold ring. He had to get to midnight without any of them noticing the flicker of desire between him and Emma.

But it was impossible to keep his eyes off her.

She was a calm, controlled center in the whirl of a festive hurricane. Directing guests to their seats and organizing the sixteen teams into the bracket. Skillfully running the first round with a sparkle in her eye, cracking up at some of the better answers the teams gave to the silly, holiday-themed prompts and keeping the crowd entertained.

Handling it, as promised.

Damn, she was impressive.

"All right, everyone, we're down to eight teams!" she announced to the crowd. "Bonus points to Brody Emerson for the unanimous winning answer of 'my cousin's beard' to the question 'things that could scrub Santa's sleigh.'"

The crowd laughed and Luke gave them a wave while balling up a list of used questions and chucking it at his cousin's head.

Brody grinned and slung his arm over the back of Bea's chair.

Luke was about to announce the start of round two when one of the competitors sitting across from Brody, Aleja Brooks Flores, lurched to her feet. Her tawny face looked as green as the elf-hat thing stuck to Emma's headband.

"Oh, no!" Aleja slapped a hand over her mouth and ran out the door, presumably in the direction of the bathroom.

Murmurs ran through the crowd.

Emma's sister Nora rose from her seat. "I'll go check on her."

Luke caught Emma's gaze and raised his brows, mouthing, *Delay*?

"Looks like we'll be taking a five-minute break before round two, folks," Emma said into her microphone. She turned it off. "That didn't look good."

"Nope."

She pulled her phone out of her pocket. "Oh, crap."

"What?"

She made a face. "Nora says, 'Looks like we won't be going for the triple crown this year.'"

Locals often tried to win the shelter construction, animal call and trivia competitions, earning bragging rights for the following twelve months. Aleja and Nora had held the title more than once.

"Crap." Luke glanced around the room and

flicked the mic back on. "Change of plans, every-one. We have a team who needs to bow out of round two. Should we draw names out of a hat to bring back one of the losing teams?"

"No!" someone from the crowd shouted. One of Emma's many cousins, by the looks of it. "You and Emma need to compete."

Warmth crept up his neck. The next round had the teams scribbling out fake definitions for words on signs, and the crowd voted with their phones. That was a lot of words to misspell.

"Wouldn't be fair for us to participate," he said. "House advantage."

"Not unless you memorized all the Christmas Balderdash cards," Brody said with a raised voice.

If he'd known he was going to get called on to compete, he would have done exactly that.

Luke took a breath and ran through his mental list of strategies for dealing with his learning disability. "Could you do the writing?" he asked Emma.

"Yes, but—"

Brody stood up. "What do you say? Should the hosts put their money where their mouths are?"

He was going to kill his cousin.

Brody strutted through life like he was always standing on a gold medal podium. He had enough of the hardware, having been on championship crews in every national and international competition in exis-tence. And he meant well, but he sometimes forgot winning didn't come as easy for everyone.

The audience cheered, hooting in approval.

Which was a good thing. The whole point of the night was for everyone to have a good time. And nobody who mattered gave a damn his brain processed things differently.

"All right. What the public demands, the public gets," Luke said into the microphone.

"Luke," Emma whispered. "We can't."

"Thought you weren't a quitter, Emma," he replied, matching her quiet volume.

"I'm *not*."

Unless she thought he wasn't going to be a good teammate... The possibility poked him in the impossible-to-harden spot, worn raw every time he stumbled over a sentence in elementary school.

"You worried I'll hold you back from victory?"

"No!" She rested a hand on his forearm, gaze sincere. "I just think someone who doesn't work here needs to win the prize."

Relief melted through him. "I wouldn't worry about it. We'll make sure we lose in this next round."

She drew back. "Lose?"

"Yeah, if you're that opposed to playing games with me," he said.

And if there was some suggestion in his tone, well, she deserved it.

"I'll show you 'playing games,' Luke Emerson."

Laughter erupted in the crowd.

Emma stiffened, face reddening. She forced a smile for the chuckling guests.

"Live mic, honey," he said casually. At least everyone watching would see the same thing they always did—Luke and Emma bickering, looking decidedly like people who didn't like each other.

He fully intended to make sure they didn't progress to the next round. Getting Emma to blush a few more times tonight would be enough of a win.

An hour and a half later, Luke sat next to Emma as the crowd applauded the two teams going on to the final round.

He nudged his reluctant partner with an elbow. "Apparently, we need to add 'expert knowledge of ridiculous holiday trivia' to our résumés."

She glowered at him from behind her cat-eye glasses. They made her look like a librarian hiding a secret filthy side. A filthy librarian with a penchant for holiday accessories, given her silly headband.

"I feel terrible we're in the finals," she said. "We're the hosts. It's not right, no matter how much the crowd wants it."

"Told you we should try to lose."

"I can't purposefully lose, Luke. God. You were an athlete. You should understand competition."

"Being an athlete is what *taught me* about losing," he muttered.

Eyes wide, she froze.

He lifted an eyebrow and waited for her to toss a platitude at him. Or pity, acknowledging how he'd fallen short. She couldn't say anything to him he hadn't already heard from scouts or the management of the pro team that had let him go. From his ex-fiancée.

From himself.

"Let's focus," she said. "Not that we have a chance against Bea and Brody in a freaking Newlywed Game. They know more about each other than your average married couple."

"Why do you think I didn't want to get this far?" He glanced at the projector screen, where the final round's theme—All I Want for Christmas Is You— was splashed in bold script. He knew what it said, though the curvy font made his vision swim a little. He leaned into the microphone. "It's not right for Emma and me to compete in the final, being the organizers. The third-place team can have our place."

The crowd replied with disappointed groans.

"No backing out now," Hank announced from the doorway. He shuffled past and sat in one of the armchairs next to the hearth.

"Grandpa! You made it," Brody said.

Oh, now Luke's cousin was really going to die. "You invited him? It's almost midnight."

"Exactly," Hank said. "Get to it! The people demand a winner. Emerson versus Emerson. Fitting, being it could be the final fifth day of Christmas."

Final. Luke's gut bottomed out. How could his grandfather say those words so calmly?

"Stop frowning and give the crowd what they want, son."

Get it together. Luke slapped on a smile.

Bea passed around the pens and the stacks of white cards.

Gripping the Sharpie, reality struck. He'd been too distracted by his grandfather's appearance and their slim chances of winning to consider the round's format.

"Problem," he said, wincing at Emma. "This game's going to require both of us to write things down, which won't work. Not if we want my answers to say what I want them to say in the ten-second time limit. Unless… Hang on, I could get someone to scribe for me." He leaned into the mic. "Anyone feel like showing off their handwriting? I need to borrow you."

Confused noises came from the audience.

Crapping the bed in a nationally televised championship series had been good for one thing: it made it no big deal to talk about his learning disability in public.

"I'm dyslexic," he explained. "And my cousin already has enough of an advantage by being paired up with his best friend."

A few chuckles rose, and Graydon Halloran stood and shuffled out of his row. "I'll lend a hand. Literally." Passing by Bea, he snatched her headband, an elf hat matching Emma's, and slid it over his blond hair.

"Hey! Ringer!" Bea complained.

"I won't say a word," Gray promised.

Luke let out a relieved breath. Now that they had gotten this far, he really wanted to win for Emma, even though he had no intention of keeping the prize. But knowing more about her than Brody and Bea knew about each other was a tough order.

They got set up, standing at four podiums. He and

Gray had to look ridiculous, two big dudes squished together behind a wooden stand, but this way, he knew his answers would be recorded correctly.

The banquet captain had taken over MC duties from Emma. She announced there would be five rounds, going back and forth between the partners.

"I'll guess for you first," Emma offered, getting ready with her pen.

Bea and Brody were cracking their knuckles and grandstanding behind the podiums on the other side of the low stage in front of the fireplace.

He laughed resignedly. There was wanting to win, and there was reality. This was going to be a blowout.

"What item is at the top of your partner's Christmas list this year?" the MC asked.

Crap. He and Emma hadn't talked about wish lists. He'd have to lob her an easy one.

"Fishing gear," he muttered at Gray, who dutifully wrote the answer in bold, block writing.

"Aaaaand answers?" the MC said.

Bea flipped over "a nap," precisely matching Brody's scribbled answer. They grinned at each other.

Figured. Brody was always up with the sun, coaching rowing at the Seattle university that had snapped him up after he'd retired from a gilded competitive career.

Luke flipped over his own answer, earning a beam from Emma.

She'd written "fly-tying supplies."

He shot her a look, letting her see his surprise.

She shrugged, but her cheeks were pink.

"Close enough—I'll count it!" the MC said.

It was his turn. His neck heated. He'd love to blame the fire roaring in the hearth behind them, but it was all nerves.

"What does your partner consider to be the best part of the holidays?"

Oh, easy. "Family traditions," he said to Gray.

When Emma flipped over her card, a victorious jolt ran up his spine. He'd gotten the answer exactly right.

His cousin, not so much.

"What? *Poinsettias?*" Bea shrieked, flicking her card at Brody like a Frisbee. "How could you not know it's the glitter for me? The lights everywhere, the colors. God, Brody."

"You're a florist," Brody mumbled, plucking the discarded answer off the floor. A wistful, knowing look crossed his cousin's face, as if he knew the answer full well, but had written the wrong answer on purpose.

Luke rolled his eyes. Those two would never make sense to him.

Emma got Luke's next answer right—favorite food, Grandma's stuffing.

"You seemed to like it the other night," she explained, gaze darting everywhere but Luke's face.

"Next up," the MC said, "what winter activity does your partner love the most?"

Damn. If he had a minute, he'd have been able to reason his way through it better. With only ten seconds, he wasn't sure. "Put 'not building snow forts.'"

Gray snorted and wrote down Luke's answer. "Snowmobiling," he said, not moving his lips.

Emma flipped her card over. "Snowmobiling."

"Seriously?" Luke said, exposing his own answer.

A mix of laughter and groans erupted from the crowd.

Hands on her hips, she glared at him.

"All right, we're all tied!" the MC announced. "Fifth answer is the winner. Favorite childhood Christmas memory."

Luke's heart stuttered. No matter how much he wanted to lie about this one, come up with some falsehood like opening stockings or second helpings of ham and turkey, he couldn't. His grandfather knew the answer, and if Luke lied, Hank would wonder why. Every year the lake froze over, Luke put on his new skates and played pick-up hockey with his grandpa until it was time for dinner.

Swallowing, Luke cupped his hand around his mouth and said, "Trying out my new skates."

Indecision swamped Emma's gaze. She tugged her glossy red lower lip between her teeth and dashed out her answer.

"Brody, what's your answer?" the MC said.

Brody held up his card, calling out, "Grandma's cooking."

Turning as white as a sheet, Bea folded her card up and clutched the clump of paper in a fist. "I was, uh, way off."

Everyone looked at her, seemingly curious as to why she wouldn't show off her answer.

The paper shook in Emma's hand. She was still biting her lip.

"It's all good," Luke told her, turning over his card and showing the crowd.

His grandfather's mouth softened in a nostalgic smile.

"Oh!" Emma squeaked. "I was right!"

Her card read "skating on the lake."

He couldn't stop his jaw from dropping. Did she understand him that well?

"How did you know?" he said in her ear, leaning in close to be heard over the cheers and applause rocking the room.

"It's your grandpa's favorite memory, too. He's mentioned it more than once. I took a chance it mattered to you, too," she said.

Something wobbled in Luke's chest. Not only from learning that something he and his grandpa had shared mattered so much to the older man, but realizing Emma had remembered it. And how she seemed to have several facts about Luke filed away.

He rubbed a hand along his beard and accepted the microphone from the MC.

"Thanks for coming, everyone. Emma and I will happily lord our victory over our family members."

Everyone laughed.

Luke forced a smile. If Emma got her way, bought the lodge and chose not to run the festival, their win would be the last one.

He didn't announce that to the crowd. No need to bring down the mood.

He pulled the box with the ring from the pocket of his jeans. "The ring is Bea's, since she's the only one not running the event or related to the owner."

Bea was nowhere to be seen. Where had she disappeared to? His cousin stood behind his podium, face blank. Luke handed him the box. "Can you give this to her?"

Emma's hand landed on his arm. "I think I need to find my sister."

"Of course." He gave her a quick squeeze on the shoulder, then thanked the crowd for coming and reminded them to drive safe.

An hour later, the place was back to normal, tables arranged for breakfast service.

Emma, who'd returned a while ago from talking to Bea, was fussing with centerpieces. Every once in a while, he caught her looking at him.

"Emma?" he said.

"Yeah?" She didn't look up from the flower she was carefully floating in a tall, cylindrical vase on the buffet table.

Not a familiar vase. "Where'd that come from?"

"Brought it with me," she said.

It looked out of place in the rustic room.

A storm cloud in the form of his cousin blasted through the kitchen doors, interrupting before Luke could point out the dining room would look silly done up like a fancy-ass banquet hall.

"Bea doesn't need this." Brody tossed the ring box to the table nearest to Luke. It clunked, bounced and landed on the ground.

Luke snatched it up. "What happened?"

"I went to find her, figure out what the hell made her look like a ghost."

"Which was…"

Brody scrubbed his face with both hands. "She'd written 'when Dad was home for the holidays.' Jesus, am I glad she crumpled her card up. If Grandpa had seen it, or my mom…"

"Or you," Luke said quietly.

Sandy-blond eyebrows arched at him. "I'm not going to collapse every time my dad's mentioned."

"Sure, whatever," Luke said. If his cousin needed to pretend he'd been okay since the day he'd opened the door as a ten-year-old kid and found two uniformed army personnel on his porch, so be it. "What about Bea, though? Why doesn't she want the prize?"

"She already has a ring."

"Huh?"

"Her boyfriend just showed up. *Fiancé*, I should say." Brody spat the words. "Proposed to her under the light walk arch with a diamond the size of my fist."

"And you have a problem with the guy?" *Or with Bea getting engaged at all?*

"Jason is a dick. Bea needs someone who understands how magical she is, and that asshole does not." Brody raked a hand through his hair. "Whatever. I'll go check on Grandpa."

He stormed out the door to the balcony. A gust of cold air blew into the room.

"Your sister, engaged. Good times," he said to Emma.

"Yeah. Good times." She sounded as excited about the prospect as Brody. She rubbed her hands over her bare arms.

Her flimsy, sequined tank top should have come with a warning label. So much skin, exposed, begging for his touch.

"Most people wear sweaters in December." His attempt at being a smart-ass came out a croak.

She bristled and strutted over to the mantel. Fingers busy straightening the tinsel, she called out, "Friday night calls for some glitter and glam."

Not seeing anything else that needed fixing—the rest of the staff had taken care of it all—he slung himself into one of the armchairs in front of the fireplace. A few last embers glowed on the grate.

"You had some good guesses in the last round," he said.

"They weren't guesses. I pay attention," she said. "It's important to pay attention to the people around you."

"Even the ones you don't like?"

She whirled, accidentally taking a strand of garland with her. It hung from her clenched fist like a tail ripped off a kid's stuffed animal. "I didn't say I didn't like you."

He chuckled. "You never acted like you did."

"You called me a snob!"

"I'm sorry. I know the 'I was a stupid kid' excuse falls flat, but I sure wasn't smart back then."

Her gaze narrowed and she perched on the arm of the chair across from him. "You were too smart."

"Not with dating, honey."

"Ugh, who is?" Face crumpling, she crossed her arms over her chest. He didn't think it was because of the chill in the room. "Even my flighty little sister can manage to find an investment banker who flies across three states for one night to propose to her. And I try so hard. For nothing."

"Do you try *too* hard?"

Her back snapped straight. "What?"

"You're so focused on finding some idealized love. Getting close to someone means being okay with their flaws. Being okay with your own."

"Oh, and you're all-knowing about this?"

"When it comes to not measuring up in a relationship?" He sighed. "Me failing out of hockey didn't work for Cara."

Emma's face shifted between fury and self-defense. "I'd never break up with someone because they didn't make the NHL."

"But you'd break up with a guy who didn't say 'I love you' on whatever arbitrary schedule you have in your head."

She shot to her feet so fast she had to hold up a hand to stop her glasses from sliding off her nose. "You've gone, what, ten years without saying 'I love you' to a woman?"

His neck tingled. "Says who?"

"Gossip? An educated guess? Does it matter if it's true?"

He scowled.

"It *is* true, right?"

"Yes."

Victory lit her eyes. "So, you don't get to have an opinion on when and how I want the man I'm with to be open about his feelings."

"It's not my 'opinion,' Em. It's a fact. You look for flaws in the man you're with."

"Let me guess, you have some theory on *why* I do that." She held up a finger. "Why you *think* I do that, I mean. Because I don't."

He pinched the bridge of his nose. "You being in love with love is not a state secret."

"I am n—*argh*!"

"If the high heel fits, wear it, Emma." He crossed his arms and glanced at her spangly stilts. "Unless you're at an outdoor lodge. Then it's a damn health and safety hazard."

He could have sworn he heard her growl.

"I'm dressed in a perfectly appropriate manner for tonight's event." She pointed a finger at him. "And I had good reasons for ending the relationships I've been in."

"Debatable."

"You know what?" She backed away a step, fists balled at her sides. "I liked you better when you were kissing me."

Whirling, she took off for the door.

"So, why did you stop?" he called after her. He sure hadn't wanted to pull away from her soft mouth, from learning the weight of her in his arms. Ridiculous, really. They could barely have a conversation without arguing.

You don't need words to kiss.

He couldn't help the laugh that escaped.

Why did I stop?
Because you're an ass, Luke Emerson.

Laughing at her.

Having one or two serious boyfriends a year wasn't anything unusual, nor was discovering perfectly good reasons for breaking things off with them. *Luke* was the one who couldn't manage being in a relationship, not her.

It was only a fifty-yard walk from the back entrance of the lodge to the cabin Hank had insisted she stay in, but without a jacket, each step bit into her skin. She hurried down the path, wincing as snow slopped into her shoes.

Hand shaking, she fumbled to get her key out of her pants pocket and into the lock.

"Emma!" Luke jogged onto the porch. "Damn it, what do you have against wearing a jacket outside?"

"You don't have one on," she pointed out.

"Yeah, and I'm freezing."

"Good. You deserve it."

The key clattered across the lock.

"Hey." He cuddled against her back, his hard body sheltering her from the chill. The scent of woodsy, warm man swirled around her. Argh, why did being close to him feel so good? Nothing else about him meshed with her. He questioned her in ways no one had, made assumptions about her that no one did... Made her question herself. *Was* she the one at fault for never finding someone to last the long haul?

How dare he?

It took all her willpower not to plant an elbow in his navel. "You *laughed* at me."

"No, I didn't." He sounded aghast.

"Then what was so freaking funny?"

His work-roughened palm rasped against the back of her hand, guiding the key and unlocking the door. "I was laughing at myself."

"Why?" She spun in his arms. The cold wood of the door chilled her back through her thin sleeveless blouse. She bowed away from the frigid planks, only managing to bring her body closer to his muscled frame, her hips pressing to his. Not just her movement, though. His hands slid around her waist, pulling her closer.

"Because this feels too good."

She put a palm to his chest. "You aren't making sense. Either you think I'm a fool for wanting to be in love or you want to kiss me. It can't be both."

"I don't think you're a fool." His voice was a soft caress. "Just reckless. Being vulnerable usually ends with your heart getting ripped out." Fingers slid along her skin, one up her neck, burying in her hair, another in the dip between her shoulder blades, exposed by her top. His lips followed. His murmur was barely audible. "And you make me want to tear my hair out sometimes. But also, to kiss you. Kiss you without stopping."

The incongruity swirled around her, mixing with the heat of his body and the chill of the air. She should hate all his unwanted opinions. Hate how right he was.

Restless need coursed through her. She whimpered as his fingertip caressed the tender skin behind her ear. She arched into him, her sensitive breasts begging for friction. "I can't think straight when I'm with you."

"Honey, you're…"

His mouth landed on hers, hot, insistent. Tongue and lips and his delicious taste, the one she wanted on her tongue before her morning coffee. She could run with that feeling, let herself imagine his hot mouth tracing a slow trail over her collarbone, between her breasts.

Uh-oh. "We need to think this through."

"Stop?" His forehead rested against the top of her head. His panting breaths teased her skin.

"No. Just pause."

"Okay." A soft kiss brushed her forehead. "I'll see you in morning."

"Yes. Of course." Her heart was still thrumming. "Snowshoeing. Uh, have a good sleep."

He leaned toward her ear. "Sleep? After this? I doubt it."

She traced a hand down his bearded cheek, her body protesting as she peeled herself away from his gorgeous frame. His gray gaze was magnetic, pulling the truth from her.

"I doubt it, too."

Chapter Seven

Emma trudged toward the marshaling area the next morning, borrowed snowshoes hugged to her chest. Her legs were heavy from lack of sleep. She squinted at the milling crowd. About fifty or so people were either wearing or carrying snowshoes, faces bright for a morning jaunt through the snow.

And there were, naturally, the six geese.

Not exactly "a-laying." More like "eating snow and eyeing people suspiciously from their enclosure."

Part of her family's egg-laying flock, borrowed annually to add to the ambiance, perched amongst hay bales. Hopefully none of the lodge guests were hungry hunters. The half dozen geese were as attached to the family as dogs.

One of them waddled over to the fence and honked at her as she passed.

"Popular with the domesticated bird population?" Luke's voice, tinged with amusement, came from behind her. He carried a clipboard in one hand and had his webbed snowshoes tucked under his other arm. His green Santa hat tilted jauntily on his head.

He was wearing it again. Her mouth curved up.

Damn it. It was safer to still be mad at him for poking at her about her relationship history last night. For how she couldn't get his kiss, his touch, out of her thoughts. It had been a long time since she craved a man's kiss the way she craved Luke's.

Not good.

"You get your gun-happy eyes off my family's pets," she said, keeping her tone light.

Even so, his face fell.

"I would never—"

"I know, Luke." She closed her eyes, regretting how slow her brain was moving this morning. Throughout the night, she'd been plagued by restless, light sleep, too-hot limbs, a whirling mind. It had finally faded at some point in the wee hours. But the fog that had rolled in in its place was clouding her mind. "Sorry. I was kidding."

The goose nearest the fence examined Luke with beady eyes and honked again.

"Did that goose swear at me?" he asked.

"She was wishing you season's greetings."

"Threatening to dress *me* up like a Christmas goose, is more like it." He stifled a yawn.

Emma must have looked more concerned than she intended because his expression turned mischievous.

"Told you I wasn't going to sleep well."

Her cheeks heated. "Are you still planning to lead the snowshoe pack?"

"Yup. It's tradition."

Out of the corner of her eye, she noticed a couple of her Brownies, the twins, kneeling by the goose fencing.

"Careful," she warned. "They're friendly, but don't stick things through the fencing. Especially not your fingers."

The sisters nodded. "Is our tree winning, Ms. Emma?" Addie asked.

"Not sure, sweetie." She glanced at Luke.

He smiled at the girl. "Can't give away the leaders yet, but you've gotten lots of votes."

The twins grinned and started honking softly at the birds.

Emma chuckled and refocused on Luke. "You wanted me to bring up the rear, right? Or do you want me to join you at the front since I know the property?" The fun-run-style race—tromp, really— traversed onto Halloran ranch property, along one of the rarely used backroads that stayed unplowed in the winter.

Luke stroked a gloved thumb down her cheek. "If you want to lead with me, I can ask Brody to be the caboose."

"I don't know. It's been a long time since I went

snowshoeing and I don't want to make a mistake somehow."

"Hey. Today's about fun. We're allowed to have some, too, you know," he said.

An early jog in the snow came nowhere near the top of Emma's list of fun things to do on a Saturday morning.

She could, however, think of a few fun things to do with the man next to her. Things to do *to* him.

Maybe she'd steered clear of him for this very reason. Avoiding him wasn't all about the disdain he'd held for her for so long. It was because under that disdain, a powerful, exceedingly problematic pull existed between them.

Find someone who makes you feel alive, Emma.

She shook her head at the memory. Grammy hadn't meant someone completely Emma's opposite. She opened her mouth to say something inane, but a pair of honks interrupted her.

Two fat, feathered bodies wedged themselves between her and Luke, forcing Luke to back away. They started hissing and nipping at him.

"Holy hell!" Luke took off through the knee-deep snow, the geese hot on his heels and making a racket.

"Damn it. Nora?" Her sister was nowhere to be seen. Emma rushed over to the fence, where the twins had opened a hole big enough for a goose to get through. She quickly closed the hole before another bird could escape.

"Girls, it's dangerous to let the birds out. They could get hurt, or hurt people."

"Warden Luke likes birds. He works with them," Addie reasoned. Her brown eyes were wide with worry under her striped beanie.

Emma peered above the crowd, trying to get a sightline on Luke. He was a basketball court's distance down the snowy backroad, the birds in hot pursuit. Must have been a pair of the geese Emma helped raise when she lived at home; geese had long lifespans and memories and bonded with their owners. Got downright territorial, in fact.

Neither goose was at all interested in bonding with Luke.

His Santa hat flew off. One of the geese stopped to bite at it. The other continued in hot pursuit.

"You could have told me you wanted to get a head start," she yelled at him, earning laughs from the crowd who were strapping into their snowshoes and warming up their limbs.

She shuffled the sheepish-faced twins away from the fence and back toward their parents. "Go get ready for the race. I need to help the warden."

Down the road, he crouched awkwardly, trying to stay out of beak range. Not so easy to do without the snowshoes he'd dropped middash, it seemed. Emma wasn't going to make the same mistake. She fixed her feet into the contraptions—ugh, she was not a natural at this—and jogged past the crowd.

She noticed her sister coming toward them from the direction of the lodge and waved for her to speed up. "Nora! The wildlife expert needs rescuing from the wildlife."

Luke's face darkened. "I'm trying to keep them away from the crowd!"

"They're harmless," Emma called to him.

The second bird pooped on the abandoned Santa hat and turned a menacing gaze on Luke.

"Harmless? Liar!" He backed away another step.

Emma snorted, picking up her pace. Her snowshoes whumped in the powder. No one deserved a goose bite, not even an infuriating man who threw out accusations like poison darts and followed that up with mind-melting kisses.

Something caught her toe, and she pitched forward. She barely got her hands out before she pancaked into the two feet of frozen fluff. Snow filled her mouth. Embarrassment flooded her veins, shocking hot in contrast to the snow creeping down her collar. A dull ache throbbed in her ankle.

For crying out loud. This was two times too many she'd been facedown in the snow this week. In front of people she cared about, too. People for whom she wanted to project a freaking base level of competence. Her ears buzzed, turning the good-natured laughs into a cascade of canned-television laughter. A couple of voices cut through the crowd noise. Nora's, calling out that she'd rescue the geese. Luke's, too.

"Graceful," he teased gently. "You okay?"

She got to her knees, spitting snow and brushing off her coat. "Of course I am."

Except for her pride, and the nagging pinch in her right ankle. *Crap.*

She'd torn up her left ankle playing rec-league

volleyball in college, to the point of needing surgery. She knew what major damage felt like, and this was nothing close to an emergency. Still, she'd have to hide it. Gritting her teeth, she held out her hands for him to help her up.

He obliged. "And here I thought snowshoes were more stable than stilettos."

"Not for me," she grumbled. "If I'd had heels on, I wouldn't have fallen."

Nora walked past, a goose honking happily under each of her arms. "Next year, you're going to need fake geese, Luke."

He blanched.

Emma could read his thoughts so easily. *Not if your sister's in charge.*

Would promising to hold the festival help to convince him to consider her offer?

Worth considering.

She ignored her smarting ankle as she and Luke led the group down the road.

"Are we going fast enough?" she said.

"*Fun*, Halloran. This crowd's more beer-league hockey and short-little-kid legs than career athletes."

"You've clearly never been out for a hike with a bunch of short-little-kid legs," she joked. "They'll run loops around you."

"I haven't," he admitted. "And I think it's cute you have, honey."

"You keep calling me that." It didn't make sense.

"I do." He sounded bemused.

"Why?"

"Maybe I think you're sweet."

She didn't know whether to growl or melt.

Focus, Emma. "If I promised to continue holding the Twelve Days festival, would you take my purchase offer more seriously? I can't commit to holding all twelve days in a row—I'd have to give priority to wedding bookings. But if I sprinkled the days throughout December…"

He stumbled, righting himself in time to avoid mimicking Emma's earlier bail.

"Lucky," she said. "Those hockey player reflexes."

"I haven't been a hockey player for twelve years." He cleared his throat and settled back into his easy rhythm. "And no, the promise of the Christmas festival isn't enough, Emma."

"I don't get it."

His gaze dropped from the winter-blue horizon to the snowy path. "My job and my family. Both are tied to this lodge, to what my grandfather has established."

"So why aren't you taking over for him? If you want the place to stay the same."

He lengthened his stride, and she had to speed up to keep pace. The pinch in her ankle deepened. She gritted her teeth and kept up. They approached her parents' property line. Morning sun glinted off the pristine stretch of white ahead. Behind them, a soundtrack of cheerful chatter and swooshing snow gear cut through what would have been silence.

"I offered to take the place over," he said finally.

Oh. Strange. Why had the older man turned Luke down? He made no bones about loving his grandsons.

Then again, what was it he'd said to Luke the other day…? *Event planning is out of your wheelhouse.*

Ouch. She didn't like the idea of Luke in charge— she wanted to run the place. But she didn't like his forced, blank expression, either.

"Wait, he didn't turn you down because of your dyslexia, did he?"

"No." He paused. "Should he have?"

"No! Why would you think I—"

"You sure never clamored to partner up with me in school."

Her cheeks, already warm from exercise, felt like she'd stuck her face two inches from a fireplace. She couldn't make an excuse about this. "I didn't want you to figure out I liked it when you flirted with me."

The corner of his mouth twitched. "Good to know."

Try the *last* thing she needed him knowing.

She narrowed her eyes, huffing from exertion. "Why else would he say no?"

"Because I've never given him a reason to say yes."

"What does that mean?"

He swore under his breath.

"I'm good at listening, if you need to talk about it," she offered quietly.

"I… It won't help, Emma."

He was wrong. But pushing would be a waste of breath.

They didn't talk much for the rest of the loop.

Emma, in part, because by the end her ankle felt like it was on fire. It took all her effort not to limp while distributing participant medals and sending the geese safely back to the ranch with Nora. Finally, she was able to remove her snowshoes and flop into a snowbank.

Luke motioned toward the lodge. "Aren't you coming?"

"Nah. It's a beautiful day. I'm going to sit and enjoy the sun." Until he was gone, so she could favor her joint like it was begging her to do.

He crossed his arms. "How much pain are you in?"

She forced an innocent look. "Pain?"

Shaking his head, he knelt by her foot and started to unlace her boot.

"Hey!"

"Let me take a look," he said.

"No. It's fine." Her foot was probably all sweaty—

"You were hobbling the whole time we were out there."

He eased off her boot and rested her foot on his knees. He peeled down her sock to her heel. The cold air hitting her swollen joint both shocked and soothed.

"Damn, Emma." He let out a hiss. "You need to get ice on this."

One swift motion, and he had her swept up in his arms.

She flung her arms around his neck and squealed.

"You can't carry me around! What will everyone think?"

"That you're too stubborn for your own good."

"Argh!" She swatted his shoulder, refusing to snuggle in because even though it would make it more comfortable, it would look ten times worse. "What about our equipment?"

"Your brother can bring it for us."

"Gray's still here?" She looked around frantically, her gaze landing on him as he approached from down the road. Crap. She did not need to be getting grief from her little brother about being carted back to the lodge by Luke.

As she'd suspected, Gray wore an up-to-no-good expression. He held up his phone.

"Do not take a picture," she scolded him.

"Too late!" he called back.

Luke set off in the direction of the lodge. Emma held on tighter. Humiliation burned through her.

But she couldn't remember the last time she'd felt so secure.

"Relax," he said. "I've got you."

The low promise rumbled through her body.

She believed it.

And worse, she liked it.

Luke shook his head at the wiggling woman in his arms. She kept shifting to look over his shoulder. To glare at her brother, no doubt.

She smelled like fresh snow and sunshine, a fragrance he'd take any day over store-bought perfume.

Though he was getting mighty attached to her sugar-lemon shampoo.

"Will you put me down already?"

"Your ankle is swollen," he said. "Which is nothing to mess with."

Gray Halloran, carrying an armful of snowshoes and Emma's boot, caught up to them and looked over in concern. "The one you hurt in college, Em?"

"No, the other one. It's minor. I'll ice it a bit before checking in on the swan swim arrangements and dropping by the Saturday happy hour."

"You're not doing anything for the rest of the day," Luke said.

"Since when are you the boss?"

He wasn't.

Wouldn't be, either. He'd told Emma the truth—he had offered to run the place on Hank's behalf. Hank had refused. *You'd be miserable, son. All the paperwork and business parts—you'd hate sitting at a computer all day. And I won't let you live the rest of your life resenting the lodge I love so much.*

Hank was right.

He was also full of BS. Yeah, Luke loved how his job meant spending most of his days outdoors. He was also entirely willing to sacrifice that for the lodge, and Hank knew it. No, it had to do with Hank not trusting Luke to follow through, to be successful in following in the Emerson footsteps.

Heart aching, he climbed the two stairs to the porch on Emma's side of the cabin.

"Let me down," she complained.

"Wait," Gray said, still following. "I need a picture of you two crossing the threshold. Jack and Bea missed out on all this today. It'll be endless entertainment for Christmas dinner." He snapped a shot.

"It's not a freaking threshold!" Emma protested. "Let me down, please."

Luke did, but she wobbled on her one booted foot, and ended up clinging to him again.

All her firm curves fit just right against him.

Do not react. Do not.

"Jack's home?" He'd done some wildland firefighting with Gray and Emma's cousin in his posthockey summers.

"Yeah. Not for long, though. He's flying back to be with his girlfriend on Christmas Eve," Emma said as she opened the door. She minced forward.

"For Christ's sake," he said, scooping her up again and carrying her inside.

She squealed.

"Now, *that* was the threshold," Gray said, busting a gut.

Luke kicked the door shut before Emma could wiggle from his grasp and tackle her brother. "Chair or bed?"

"Chair," she said.

He settled her into one of the armchairs by the fireplace. She'd covered the olive green fabric with a plaid blanket he didn't recognize.

"What's with the blanket?"

"I've been trying out some decorating." She shifted and propped her injured ankle on the footstool.

He glanced around the room. Come to think of it, it did look different. A few small vases of flowers dotted the mantel. She'd rearranged the small table and created a simple centerpiece for it, similar to the vases she'd been working on in the dining hall. She'd switched out the bedding on the king-size bed, too—instead of the utilitarian beige, it was cream with a delicate gold stripe.

"You've been busy."

"Yeah." She leaned forward, wincing as she rubbed her ankle. "I'm going to do it up to show Hank. These cabins could look super romantic with the right touches."

Luke made a face. "No one needs a fussy room when they come to fish or rock climb."

She sighed and prodded her ankle gingerly.

No retort? Huh.

"I don't think there's any ice in the mini-fridge," she said.

"I'll go get what we need from the lodge."

The main building was humming with midday activity. He retrieved an ice pack and tensor bandage from the medical room and headed for the buffet. Nodding greetings to a few guests he recognized, he balanced the food on a tray: two coffees, an assortment of sandwiches and a couple of the gooey peppermint brownies his grandma had perfected when he was a kid. The cook got them close, but they always lacked a bit of the Jenny Emerson magic he remembered. He made his way back to the cabin carefully, not wanting to dump his spoils on the ground.

The front room was empty when he let himself in. Running water hissed behind the closed bathroom door. *The shower.*

A flash of irritation blitzed through him. She shouldn't be standing until she iced for a while. Could she seriously not sit still for ten minutes?

Setting the tray on the table, he took a deep breath and tried to think of anything except water running over Emma's smooth limbs.

Yeah, not happening.

Rivulets of water streaming over creamy skin blazed in his mind.

The room shrank to his mental picture of laying Emma out on the bed and—

Damn it. Heat rushed low, and he had to adjust his pants. He needed a shower, too. A cold one.

Chapter Eight

Luke tossed on a long-sleeved T-shirt and a pair of jeans, grimacing to himself. His half-hard length protested the stiff material. The icy shower he'd rushed back to his own cabin to take had done nothing to cool him down.

He needed to hold it together. And to hurry up. Emma had another thing coming if she thought he was going to let her scurry around checking on things that were already organized or redecorating rooms that didn't need a transformation.

He knocked quickly on the door. Opening it but keeping his gaze on the deck planking, he called out, "Emma? You decent?"

No answer.

He let himself in. The room was still empty. He

went over to the bathroom door. "Em, honey, you need to start icing."

The door flung open. A thin tank top peeked out of the V of her white bathrobe. Her dark hair was damp, loose around her shoulders. Warmth rolled out of the steamy bathroom, fogging the lenses of her glasses and flushing her face.

"Stop hovering, mother hen." She took a step to pass him and winced.

"You're going to hurt yourself worse if you keep pretending you aren't hurting." He bent down to give her a shoulder to lean on, getting her to the edge of the bed.

"The ibuprofen will kick in soon."

"Lie back," he said.

Her pupils flared at the command.

"So I can wrap your ankle," he clarified.

"I'll do it myself later." She settled onto the fluffy pillows, jamming one under her foot. "I will take the ice pack, though."

The weary look that crossed her face made him ache inside. He wrapped the ice pack in a hand towel and tucked it around her swollen ankle. No bruising— that was good, at least.

"Emma." He sat on the edge of the bed, gripping the shin of his bent leg so he wouldn't be tempted to reach for her. "Even if it's minor, it's still worth properly resting it."

She fidgeted with the edge of her robe, tugging the thick terry over her knees and covering as much of her collarbones as was physically possible. "I'm not here to rest."

"I know." His mouth curved on one side, a fonder smile than he'd intended. "You're here to prove me wrong."

"Convince you I'm right," she corrected in a soft voice. Her gaze flitted around the room. "Can't you see it? A couple, cozying up by the crackling fire after sharing some of the most important words they'll ever say… Sharing more words together, privately, surrounded by everything beautiful my great-grandfather put into these buildings when he constructed them. The lodge needs some updating, but these cabins only need to be redecorated."

"Your great-grandfather built this cabin." The reminder struck him harder than he'd expected.

"He did."

Something twisted in his chest. Her own connection to the place was almost as strong as his own. Hers was to the past, though, not the present. And the present function mattered more than dwelling on romantic nostalgia.

She crossed her arms, staring at him. Challenging him in a way he couldn't quite read. A hint of a shiver shook her.

"You're cold." He went over to the fireplace and got a fire started. Bringing the blanket back with him, he tucked it around her.

"And you're fussing."

He stroked a damp strand of hair off her forehead. "Doesn't anyone ever fuss over you?"

"Not really."

Her hand slid into his. Soft, and tipped with those sparkly nails. Strong, too, enough to split a half a cord of wood, or dig a snow shelter. Emma seemed to be able to do whatever she put her mind to.

Including erasing the best parts from your favorite place in the world.

But with their fingers laced, her plans didn't seem as pressing. He stroked his thumb along the inside of her wrist.

She let out a breathy *oh*.

"I would have thought with a big family like yours, you'd have been indulged all the time," he said.

He'd been jealous, to be honest. Being at the lodge with Grandpa and his mom. She had tried her best, but living in Montana hadn't been her thing. She was much happier in Denver with her second family, wearing suits every day and working as a paralegal. Not tearing her hair out to help him with his homework or driving him into Bozeman for hockey practice a hundred times a week, or pretending she liked ice fishing on the days she deigned to go out with Hank and him. The lodge had been busy with guests, but lonely for company. Brody had walled himself off for a lot of years after his dad died in combat, so they hadn't been close then.

And watching the Hallorans next door, two loving parents and four kids, five once Jack moved in— he'd assumed it was heaven. Still did, really. Had he misunderstood?

"Funny thing about being in the middle," Emma said quietly. "People tend not to notice when you need anything, let alone indulging."

"I saw you."

Her lips twitched. "You invited me fishing."

"Not sure if I was being overconfident or naïve." The back of his neck tingled, and he rubbed it with his free hand.

Mirth danced in her eyes. "You, at eighteen? I'd say the first."

"You thought so at the time." He dropped his gaze to their joined fingers.

"I was having a hard time thinking of anything during senior year. Staring at your shoulders, and the way your hair was an inch too long at the back, taunting me to play with it? It's a miracle I got an A in that class."

He tried to keep his mouth from gaping, but nope, it flapped open like a damn trout's. She'd been interested in him? Or at minimum, thought he was hot?

"Maybe if I'd said yes to fishing, I'd have learned how good a kisser you were. Before you inevitably broke my heart."

"Inevitably."

It was a logical assumption. He still didn't like it.

"But that good kissing part…" She tugged on his hand.

"Probably would have been a disappointment there, too," he grumbled. He flipped her hand over, cupping it in his palm, tracing patterns on the insides of her fingers with the other.

"Do you—" She sat up, knocking her ice pack off her ankle. Her cheek flinched. She leaned on a hip on the mattress in front of him, robe falling open a little, exposing a strip of pale, smooth skin.

Oh, man. The robe alone halved his chances of surviving this intact. But he couldn't walk away for the life of him.

"Do I...?"

Her mouth firmed. "Do you want to be the kind of guy who sticks?"

He clenched his fists and held them at his sides. Sitting next to her? He could manage that no problem. Pretending he wasn't getting eyestrain from looking away from the tantalizing line where her skin met her tank top? Harder, but still doable. But admit being lonely hurt less than being in a relationship? Admit he was always waiting for the inevitable moment when he'd screw up and destroy something precious? Impossible.

So he shrugged.

Pathetic, sure.

And necessary.

"Oh, no," she said. "You poked at me last night. It's only fair I get to ask you tough questions, too."

"And did you answer my questions?"

"Well, no, but—"

"Fair's fair," he said.

Her mouth pressed into a tight seam. She stood, lifted her chin a fraction and limped over to the table where he'd left the food.

She went straight for the brownie, taking a big bite and returning it to the plate.

It was a good thing she'd gotten up first, because he didn't think he had the ability, not when she'd been curled up on a bed wearing something so easy to remove. So easy to creep a hand under and explore.

Though her in white terry licking frosting off her fingers was irresistible, too.

She glanced over her shoulder, frowning. "They're not as good as your grandma's."

Easing off the mattress, he adjusted his jeans, which were getting uncomfortable again. Three lazy strides, and she was within touching range.

A bit of chocolate marked the corner of her mouth.

"They're not. Not on their own, anyway." He leaned in, licking the smudge of sweetness. "But on you…"

A sexy gasp escaped her throat.

His body heated. He craved the feeling of her breath against his skin. "Honey, every time you make that noise, I lose five IQ points."

She laughed, easy and mischievous.

Groaning, he scrubbed his hands down his face. Hell, she destroyed him.

"I don't know how good I'd be at casual fooling around," she said.

"Okay…" He drew out the end of the word. "Is fooling around even on the table?"

"It wouldn't be smart. With me wanting to buy this place, and your grandfather placing so much weight on your opinion, it's begging for complications."

"And it's hard to be perfect when things are complicated." He dipped a finger in the frosting and smeared another little dab on the corner of her mouth.

"Luke—"

He captured her complaint with his mouth. She was hot as anything, all chocolate sweet and whimpers and fingers digging into his back. Complicated, but just right in his arms.

Threading his fingers in her hair, he tilted her head back and kissed her neck. "I know a few things. How good you taste. How curious I am to know if your panties have this same lace on them."

He traced his finger along the edge of her camisole. The skin flushed pink under his touch. Flattening his hand, he spread his fingers over the bare, pretty flesh below her collarbone.

Her lips parted, and she nodded.

Slowly skidding his palm downward, under the edge of her bathrobe and over the butter-soft material of her tank, he curved his hand, ready to test the weight of her gorgeous breast.

The tip of her tongue darted out, moistening her lip.

He groaned.

Thump. Thump. Thump.

They both startled at the knock on the door. She let out a yelp and a hiss of pain.

Shifting his hands, he steadied her. "Landed on your ankle wrong?"

"Yeah."

Thump.

"For God's sake," he muttered.

Straightening her robe, she stared at him, full of beauty and spirit and smarts that he wouldn't know what to do with in a million years.

"Luke? Emma?" Hank called from the other side of the door. "You in there?"

"I'll get it," she said.

"No. Sit. You're still hurting."

He reached for the door, unsure if his grandfather's interruption had screwed up something incredible or done him the biggest favor of his life.

Emma snuggled into the corner of Hank's couch, leg outstretched and ice on her ankle like a good little soldier. Over the course of the afternoon, Luke had popped in and out to make sure neither Hank nor she was up to anything strenuous.

She'd pretended to be annoyed by his hovering. Secretly, it was nice to have a sexy, concerned man do his best to take care of her.

The cottage was a cozy place to hang out. The same wood walls of the guest cabins, with lights hanging in the windows and a real tree gracing the corner next to the TV, decked out with vintage and kitschy ornaments. She'd put it up for Hank a few weeks ago when he'd first contracted his illness.

They had on their second Christmas rom-com and

the popcorn was delicious, but sitting was driving her bananas. The pain in her ankle had receded to a dull ache, nothing she couldn't ignore. Her hands were starting to twitch from a lack of a task.

"I haven't seen this much of my grandson in days," Hank mused. Emma's cat, Splotches, was stretched out in his lap, purring shamelessly.

"Mmm." She tossed a few more buttery kernels in her mouth.

"Did I interrupt something earlier?"

"No, we were just refueling after the snowshoe." *Refueling, getting brownie kissed off my mouth— same, same.* "He was trying to boss me around and get me to sit down."

"He's overprotective." Hank's mouth scrunched. "So are you."

"When it's necessary."

"You two are more similar than you realize," Hank said.

She snorted. "We have nothing in common."

Or so she'd keep telling herself.

Hank shook his head in clear amusement.

"Hey, do you have the ingredients to make Jenny's peppermint brownies?" she asked.

"Probably, why?"

"Luke and I agreed something's missing from the lodge version. I want to figure it out."

"See, lots in common," he said with a wink. "Recipe's in the pink box in the cupboard with the sugar and flour."

Shuffling to the kitchen half of the open room,

she located the metal recipe box and dug through. "Hank, no one needs recipes for aspic or lime jelly salad with walnut dressing. *No one.*"

"Those were my mother-in-law's."

"They need to be burned." She pulled a card out, marked up with a myriad of corrections and revisions. The same script, but different inks. A one-sided conversation that had taken place over a lifetime. "Not this one, though."

An hour later, the scent of minty chocolate infused the whole front room. She had a tray of dense, rich goodness cooling on the stovetop and was whipping up frosting with a decades-old electric beater. "I'm betting one of the corrections on the recipe got missed," she mused. "Maybe the sugar measurement, or the amount of extract."

The clunk of work boots sounded on the front porch. Luke entered with a gust of cold air. Snow dusted the thick canvas of his jacket.

A few steps, and she could be brushing the flakes off his broad shoulders. Unzipping his jacket and stroking her hands up the hard, flannel-covered muscle underneath.

Getting the wits kissed out of her. He'd sure managed to do just that a few hours ago.

She clenched the handle of the knife she was using to cut the brownies.

Luke's gaze raked her from her messy ponytail to her slippered feet. He frowned. "You aren't resting."

"What's that, you don't want brownies? I guess your grandpa and I will eat them all ourselves."

Hank, fixated on the end of the movie, snorted from his armchair.

"Let's not get hasty," Luke said, toeing out of his boots and joining her in the kitchen. Stealing all the space and air and the calm she'd managed to generate while baking.

She dipped a clean spoon into the frosting, shot him an innocent look and licked the fluffy goodness with a slow sweep of her tongue. "Want some?"

His jaw clenched.

She cut him a small, warm square, spread a generous dollop of frosting on it and held it out to him.

He took it and popped it into his mouth.

Wonderment broke through the heated warning riding his face. His gray eyes widened. "You got them just right," he said around the mouthful. "How?"

Satisfaction swelled in her belly. "It's what I do. Get things right."

He stared at her, swallowing, joy fading to something unreadable.

"You know what I could also get right?" Now was as good a time to press him as any. "A public skate on day ten, if you'd stop being so stubborn."

He went rigid. "I told you Brody and I would figure something out."

"And have you?"

His jaw ticked.

"Still don't have that planned, son?" Hank said.

"We're close, Grandpa."

Not the tone of a man who was anywhere near to

a solution. "Seriously, Luke. You saw how fast I organized the *Nutcracker* night. Let me do the same for skating."

"What, and let you twist your other ankle?"

"Don't change the subject," she said. "Advertising and waivers have nothing to do with my injury."

"It'd be a hit," Hank added from his chair.

Pain darkened Luke's gray eyes. The kind that came from regret. Soul pain. "Fine, Grandpa." His gaze shifted to the floor. "You'll have to do it without me, though." He spoke quietly enough it was only for Emma.

Was his sadness over his lost hockey career, or something else? She fisted her hands, resisting the need to stroke his face, to find out what he was holding in.

"I'll get Brody to pitch in with whatever I need to organize the skate," she said. "And with the brownies, I'll compare your grandma's recipe with the one the kitchen staff is using. See if something got recorded wrong. Could also be how small and large batches end up tasting different, though."

"Or it was missing the love of a good woman," Hank threw out.

Embarrassment rushed into her cheeks.

Luke wedged himself next to her and cut off another piece, adding the frosting. Instead of popping it between his own lips, he held it in front of hers.

Accepting the treat, she chewed, savoring the sweet delight. "Mmm."

Pleasure rushed through her veins. From the brownie, not Luke's hot gaze.

"What time's the swim tomorrow?" Hank said. "I'm always first in."

Luke whirled to face his grandfather. "You have *pneumonia*."

"Exactly. I'm bored." The older man grinned. "I know I'm not swimming. I *will* bundle up and come watch. My swan hat will feel rejected if it doesn't get its annual wear."

"But—"

"It's a compromise, son."

Luke turned his attention to Emma. "How's the ankle?"

She stole another corner of brownie. "Good enough to go swimming tomorrow."

His brows rose. "You're actually going in?"

"Wouldn't miss it."

"Ground's slippery, though."

She arched a brow. She'd have thought he'd take a crack at her over the water temperature, not about a twisted joint.

"Stop worrying." She swiped a finger through the frosting and took a long, slow lick, keeping her gaze on his.

Hot promise turned his gray eyes almost black. "Emma..."

A glance toward Hank confirmed his attention was fully on the movie. Good. She didn't want the older man to see her teasing his grandson.

With the tip of her tongue, she tasted the trace of icing left on her lower lip.

Luke hissed out a breath. "Want a hand back to your cabin?"

She slowly shook her head. "I was told to rest. And I always follow instructions."

"Yeah, right."

"I will tonight." Inviting him over to finish what they'd started earlier sounded like the ultimate mistake...even if she knew it would make her holiday.

Standing behind the table where swimmers were signing and submitting waivers, Emma wrapped her oversize beach towel more tightly around herself. She'd had a perfectly nice night of icing her ankle and pretending the smell of Luke's bodywash wasn't still lingering in the air, tempting her to invite him to spread the fragrance all over the sheets.

"You're not limping anymore. And you were avoiding me last night," he murmured into her ear.

She kept her gaze on the participant she was helping and pointed at the line for the woman's signature. "Make sure you sign here."

Like the snow cave construction, it was Emma's first time attending this event. She did not plan on a repeat performance next year, not even if she kept the festival going. She'd put her own spin on the seventh day of Christmas, figure out a way to turn the swan theme into something *not* involving dunking oneself in a frigid river.

Many participants sported wet suits. She'd gone

that route, too, borrowing one from her cousin who lived on the lake and water-skied a ton during the summer. Emma doubted the neoprene would make much of a difference. Despite her winter jacket and the towel, she was shivering.

Luke wore a long-sleeved Henley, a surf-style bathing suit, wool socks and work boots.

A ridiculous getup.

Hot as hell, you mean.

His shirt left no shoulder muscle to the imagination. And since when were a guy's knees gorgeous? Luke's were—sprinkled with light brown hair, curving down into strong calves—

"See something you like, honey?"

"You're going to get frostbite." She jogged the stack of signed waivers with emphasis.

"Nah. With all these propane heaters, it's downright tropical." They had two roaring bonfires, too.

"It won't be in the river," she called after him as he strolled out from under the tent and joined his cousin at the water's edge. He and Brody had laid down a long sheet of canvas flooring to allow people a way to get in and out without slipping.

It might be nicknamed the swan swim because of the "a-swimming" line from the song, but it was going to be as polar bear–esque as any New Year's Day plunge. Snow edged the riverbank. Even though the water ran fast enough in front of the lodge to prevent it from freezing over, it wasn't warm like some of the hot springs in the area. The deeper pool in the middle the swimmers would have to dunk in to earn a swan certificate was a dark blackish green. Sometimes the river looked blue, but not with today's overcast sky.

No one else seemed to mind. The sixty-five participants, dressed up in various swan-themed hats and festive costumes over their swimming attire, blithely chattered away as they waited for the official start.

"How could a person possibly be excited about this?" Emma muttered to herself.

"It's tradition," Hank said.

She startled and went to push her glasses up, only managing to poke herself in the bridge of her nose. Right, she had her contacts in. Cheeks heating in defiance of the chill in the air, she said, "You snuck up on me!"

He grinned and adjusted his feathered bathing cap. He coughed into his elbow.

She shot him a look of concern, and he had the decency to look sheepish.

"I know, I know. As soon as I shoot the starting pistol, I'm going to head back to the house. It's a deep freeze out here today."

"You're not making me want to dive in."

Slinging an arm around her shoulders, he squeezed. "No one's saying you have to, Emma. Collecting waivers and directing traffic is just as important."

But it doesn't prove anything to Luke.

"I'll live," she said.

With a wink, Hank headed for the riverbank. He

gave a short speech, wished everyone a happy holiday and fired the opening blank. With a whoop, Brody tore into the water.

Emma glanced around, wondering if Bea had come, too.

She was nowhere to be seen. Probably sleeping in like an intelligent woman, snuggled up with her husband-to-be. Or, more likely, pitching in with ranch chores as was the usual morning routine.

Emma snorted at the thought. What would Bea's persnickety fiancé think about pig slop and cleaning horse stalls?

Come to think of it, none of her siblings were here today. Totally fine. She'd get her fill of Halloran shenanigans at their weekly Sunday dinner tonight.

The size of the pool didn't allow for a big crowd to all swim at once, so people ran in and dunked under in small groups, shrieking and laughing. No one tarried, that was for sure.

"Emma!" Brody, wearing a bathrobe and a wool hat, called from beside one of the fires. "No chickening out! You need to be the grand finale with Luke!"

"Yay!" she shouted back, forcing enthusiasm.

Her cousin Lauren, Emma's wet suit dealer, ran by on her way out of the river, hand in hand with her husband. Lauren's blond hair wasn't even dripping—it had already started to freeze. Her teeth chattered. "Hold hands, Emma—it makes it easier to get in." She winked as she hurried toward the bonfire, a steaming mug of mulled apple cider and the snuggling arms of her love.

"See?" a suggestive voice murmured in Emma's ear. "Body heat. Works like a charm."

Oof. She didn't need to be close to Luke's body to feel warm. A few low words skimming across the skin of her temple, and her blood was singing.

The sight of him shirtless didn't help matters. His bare chest and ropy, muscled arms drew her in just as much as his legs. A faded scar crossed his left biceps. *Oof. Right.* Him getting shot had been all anyone in town could talk about a few years back. Had the poacher aimed a few inches to the left...

He cocked his head. "Emma? Where'd you go?"

"Nowhere productive." She clenched her towel in her fists—it wouldn't do to reach out and trace the remnants of his old wound. "And we're *not* snuggling by a bonfire post-swim."

"Missing out, then."

She pinned him with a stare. "We'd give people the wrong idea."

He leaned in again. "As long as you and I know the score, no one else matters."

Except I don't know the score.

Nor did it feel like they were playing a game anymore.

Chapter Nine

Hoots and hollers sounded from a few people close by, encouraging Emma to jump in the river. She could swear the water was taunting her as it flowed by, gray and unforgiving. Damn it. She should have jumped in with Brody at the beginning, gotten it over with.

"Drop the towel, Halloran." Luke took her hand. His gaze wandered along her body as she revealed her wet suit-clad frame.

"Are you checking me out?" She pretended to be affronted.

"Always." He grinned. "It's go time."

"You jump first," she said.

"Nope. Together."

"You can do it, Emma!"

That sounded like Lauren. Emma couldn't be totally sure, because her heartbeat was clunking in her ears like a train accelerating out of the station.

He tugged her down to the edge. "You're shaking."

"It's cold!"

"Right." He clearly didn't believe her. "You gotta just go for it. Scale of one to ten, low being pain-free, how's your ankle feeling?"

"A two."

"A real two, or a stubborn-woman two?"

She rolled her eyes. "A real one. Promise."

"Good. Ready, honey?"

No.

She nodded. "Okay. One, two—"

A warm hand yanked her arm. She sucked in a breath but cold tore it from her lungs.

It was knives, needles, every sharp thing piercing her skin at once, seeping into the wet suit and right through to her core.

She broke the surface, ears and fingers and toes throbbing. "I didn't say three!"

Her knuckles and joints were on fire. How could cold feel like flames? Turning away from his smiling face, she swam toward the edge and crawled out, shaking worse than she had in her entire life.

Brody handed over her dry towel.

Luke splashed out of the water behind her. "And that's all, folks! Warm up those extremities, and we'll see some of you for the ice cream bar at dinner tomorrow night."

"H-how can anyone th-think of ice cr-cream

right n-now?" Every muscle in her body cramped and complained.

"A stint by the fire and you'll be back to normal," he promised.

"You're b-barely shiv-vering! J-jerk!"

He snuggled up to her and shuttled her over to the nearest propane heater. His lips curved against her forehead. "Why don't you head to the cabin to get warm? I can finish up here."

Locking her jaw to stop her teeth from chattering, she shook her head.

Stripping out of her wet suit and donning warm clothes to help with cleanup only took the edge off. She was still shivering by the time she and Luke got back to their cabin. He followed her onto her half of the porch.

A hand landed on her lower back, a delicious weight.

"Oh, you think you're coming in?" she said.

"Hoping to."

"You're going to remind me about sharing body heat, aren't you?"

"Would it work?"

The gravel of his voice scraped against her willpower. What was the point in still pretending they didn't want each other? "As long as we can keep personal separate from business."

"I think we can."

She pulled him inside her cabin.

"Good grief, I'm still so cold." She left a trail of coat, boots, fleece-lined leggings and sweater on the floor. Stripped down to her camisole and silky panties, she dove under the covers and pulled them to her chin.

Luke hovered by the doorway, still bundled in his outerwear, jaw pretty much on the floor.

She smiled, slow and teasing. "Problem?"

"Uh, no, honey. Not even a bit."

"You must be cold, too."

He rubbed a hand along the edge of his beard. "If I pretend to be, will you warm me up?"

"I might," she said.

His gray gaze went molten. He shucked his coat and unlaced his boots, all the while pinning her with that hot stare. His socks hit the floor, one at a time.

She expected the tight Henley to join them, the sweatpants, too, but he kept those on.

Her belly tightened. Him staying clothed wasn't a bad thing. Maybe she'd strip him down herself.

The mattress sagged under his weight as he slid between the covers.

She rolled into him, earning a smile from his kissable mouth.

Time lagged. A fragmentation of seconds she knew happened so rarely, of her body testing her place against his. Of too much sensation all at once, spilling over in her mind. Her skin, taking in the heat of him and the softness of his clothes and the sculpted muscle underneath. His bodywash again, fresh and clean, plus an outdoorsy tang from the river and a hint of woodsmoke. His magnetic gaze, holding her own, refusing to let go. And she knew how he tasted.

But she needed to check.

He slid one arm under her head. His other hand landed on her hip, holding her tight to his side.

Draping her knee over his thighs, she pushed her needy center against him, just enough to want more. She palmed his flat belly and teased his shirt up until her fingers found what they wanted—the sprinkling of crispy hair arrowing under the waistband of his pants. It rasped against her fingertips, like his facial hair did whenever he kissed her or pressed his cheek to hers.

Shifting on an angle, he pulled her in closer.

His thumb traced the line of her cheekbone. "Seeing you go along with the swim today—even though you were nervous as hell… Do you know how much you turned me on?"

With her leg tossed over him, she couldn't miss the truth of his admission. "Shrinkage isn't an issue, then."

"Not around you." His mouth turned up at the corner. "Not this week, anyway."

The reminder of how fast she'd gone from thinking he was the worst to having him lying next to her in her bed should have shaken her. She didn't make rash decisions. No impulsiveness, thank you very much. That was asking to have her plans derailed.

And yet, this felt unavoidable. Unstoppable.

She gripped his shirt in her fist. His heartbeat thrummed against her knuckles, echoing her own rapid pulse.

"I thought the whole point of sharing body heat

was to be naked," she said, unable to stop herself from worrying her lip. She might want this, but her hands were shaking—

He grabbed the back collar of his Henley and pulled it off, tossing it behind him.

The sheer desire in his eyes made her breath catch.

She splayed her fingers across his pecs, savoring his trimmed chest hair. She wouldn't have predicted Luke was the kind of guy to care about body hair. He clearly did, and wow, she wanted to run her lips there.

She did. His pecs. His antique-penny nipple. Over to his arm, along part of the pale streak where he'd been shot.

"Not sure kissing boo-boos works years later, but I'm not complaining." His voice was no more than a rumble.

She put her palm on his chest, soaking in the rise and fall of his quick breaths. "This was more than a scratch."

"I try not to play the what-if game," he said.

"That cocky boy I knew in high school, all convinced a puck and a stick was his fate—if someone had told him he'd turn into you, making a real difference, facing danger, caring more about wildlife and water than setting off goal lights, what would he have said?"

His gaze hardened. "Nothing worthwhile."

"Hey." It took way too many seconds of kissing

him to get his mouth to soften again. "Sorry. Didn't mean to bring down the mood."

"I love talking with you, Emma, but not while we're nearly naked."

His hands roaming her back seemed miles more important than words. "I do this sometimes. Get too into my head and forget about the moment."

"I know, honey."

A kiss landed on her neck, a rough palm on her ass, teasing the edge of her panties. Wow, he had magical hands.

She pressed closer to him. "Maybe we should go from nearly naked to regular naked."

He chuckled. "If I take my sweats off, you might end up with more than you bargained for. I didn't have underwear on with my bathing suit. Still don't."

"Oh." Locking her leg higher around his hips, she rocked. Every fraction of movement promised deeper, fuller pleasure. "But… This is exactly what I want."

"Is it?"

"Uh-huh. And I'm wearing too much, too."

"But yours is so damn sexy, sweetheart. Look at this…"

Rising on his elbow, he shifted.

She rolled. The sheets were cool under her back. "Look at what?"

A light kiss landed on the corner of her mouth. "This fallacy of a tank top…"

One rough fingertip traced a line across the thin bamboo knit, settling in the valley of her breasts, circling there, waiting. She arched her back, trying to press more of her flesh into his hand.

He chuckled. His lips teased the spot his finger had tormented.

A thumb brushed a nipple. His mouth lowered, teasing the straining peak through the fabric.

She gasped.

His hips hitched forward, pressing into the curve of her thigh. He so obviously wanted her, and the thrill of it threatened to consume her.

"No bra, sweetheart?"

"I'm pretty small."

Lifting his head, he stared at her, eyes silver with want. His big hand cupped her breast, caressing it with soul-weakening tenderness. "You're amazing."

"Thank you." Her hand slid down her belly, toward her sex. She needed more, and with him on his side and his hand on her breast, he couldn't reach—

He snagged her wrist. "Not that I wouldn't love to see you touch yourself, but right now? It's my job." His hand continued the journey hers had started. "I need to see how wet you are for me."

She froze.

So did he. "What?"

Having to explain this sometimes killed the mood… "I don't get all that wet."

He paused for a half a second and nodded. "Got any lube?"

"Yeah. In the bedside drawer."

A curious smile crept across his face.

"I use it when I'm alone, too. And lying here, thinking about you next door…"

His low groan made her feel like a sultry temptress.

He kissed the corner of her mouth. "I was doing the same."

"Good."

Reaching behind him, he snagged the little bottle from the drawer. A foil packet from his pocket followed, both placed on the sheet beside her.

"No pressure," he said. "But we have it if we need it."

"If you don't use both those things at some point very soon, I will never forgive you." She tried to smile sweetly, but her breath was coming too fast, her blood was coursing too hot.

"Emma." He kissed her, desperate lips betraying how close he was to the edge of his own control. He teased his fingertips past the edge of her panties, skimming them along her mound.

One light touch, a hint of movement along her swollen flesh.

"Don't tease me," she begged, reaching for his shoulders to pull him over her. Her hips hitched up. "I'm just… I need…"

His weight settled between her thighs.

"Yes. Better."

"Better? Not even close." Gentle fingers tugged off her camisole. He kissed where the fabric had been, laving her straining nipples. The friction from his beard tore a whimper from her.

"Luke—"

"Shh." He inched his mouth toward her navel. "You taste like a dream."

She melted against the mattress. "Mmm."

Fingers hooked her panties and stripped them off, baring her for him.

She waited for the usual twist of self-consciousness, of being fully naked and vulnerable for a man—it didn't come. How could she feel anything but worshiped when utter amazement spread on his rugged, gorgeous face?

He bent his head to her center, kissed gently, tracing her folds with his tongue.

Need cascaded through her. His tongue was perfect on her aching bud, but there was still so much emptiness, a yearning that could only be filled by being truly joined.

She wove her fingers into his soft hair. "More."

One finger, then two. Thick and wonderful.

And not what it could be.

"Luke. *More*, more."

He loomed over her, so much brawny beauty on display. His sweatpants landed somewhere on the floor, and the crinkle of a wrapper filled the air as he sheathed himself. Lube-slicked fingers danced along her folds, making her wet, ensuring her pleasure. She arched into his hand, murmuring nonsensical thanks.

"I've got you, honey. Really."

Digging her fingers into his shoulders, she begged silently for him to fill her.

Screw it, she didn't have to wait. Reaching down,

she took his thick erection in hand and stroked him, one slow caress. He was slippery, too, must have thought of prepping himself. It made it so easy to run her hand up and down his length. She smiled, learning the weight of him in her palm.

His groan was sexier than she'd thought possible.

He snagged her wrist and pinned it to the pillow.

"No more. Not this time," he panted.

Okay, all that was wildly sexy, too. This man... He could take her apart if she let him.

"I'm ready—"

"Me, too, but who's rushing?" He nudged her center, thrust slow and deep. "That feel right?"

His sweet words, the mix of passion and caring in his eyes... She hadn't expected it to be this—this much.

"It's more than right," she said, gasping on the truth.

"Good."

Another breath, another easy thrust.

"Why...why so slow?"

"I'm enjoying you, Emma." He eased in again, circling a little, hitting a just-right spot.

Her vision shimmered. Her nails had to be leaving marks on his back. He didn't seem to care.

"Luke, you're... More. Please."

She caught a glimpse of his smile as he buried his face in the crook of her neck and thrust to the hilt.

She dissolved under him. Let herself ride the wave, let it spill through every part of her body. She didn't have to hold back, didn't have to hide from pleasure and the vulnerability of release.

He stroked her hair and kissed her cheek. "Already, honey?"

Pleasure pulsed through her, and she could have sworn he got thicker, harder inside her. "I—I told you I was ready."

"Glad you enjoyed it."

"You're not done, though."

"Hell no," he said, kissing her thoroughly, stoking the embers once more. "And neither are you."

Luke had always assumed he knew what it felt like to be fully, completely sated.

Then he woke up from an indulgent Sunday afternoon nap with a naked, pleasured Emma Halloran.

Holy hell. He'd had no idea.

His limbs, heavy from sleep and the lingering hum of a powerful release. His existence, limited to languid contentment and the pliable, warm woman curved against his side. Her usual citrus kissed her skin, and the earthiness of sex. A hint of his own scent, too. Primal satisfaction rose in his belly.

She'd smack him if she knew he liked leaving his mark on her. She'd have a right to. Nothing about what they'd done suggested she was willing to be his, or to have him as hers.

Glancing at the alarm clock, he groaned.

He tightened his arms around her, kissing the top of her head. Her hair was still in the high, messy bun she'd thrown it into after the river dunk. At some point between her three orgasms, it had become adorably disheveled.

She mumbled and shifted, seeming to try to get closer. Impossible, but the effort made him smile.

"It's getting on four o'clock, honey." He kept his voice a whisper, hating to have to break their snug cocoon.

She leaped away from him as if he'd unloaded his twelve-gauge in the ceiling. Rolled in the comforter, she settled halfway across the bed.

An Emma burrito.

A *frowning* Emma burrito.

"Four?" she said. "What?"

Tugging up the sheet to his waist, he propped one of his hands behind his head and tried to look like she hadn't just ripped away his bearings.

"Problem?" he said.

Her eyes were a panicked green. "We are *not* together."

He nodded slowly. "Accurate."

So why did he hate those words on her plush, still kiss-swollen lips?

"Napping is so couple-y!"

"Says who?" he said. "Is there a nap rule book I don't know about?"

"There should be! So people don't get the wrong idea."

"What people are you talking about here, Emma?" He breathed, trying to loosen the nerves pulling at his chest. "The only people who know anything about this—the sex and the napping—are you and me."

"Uh-huh."

He lifted his brows. "And why would either of us be getting the 'wrong idea'?"

She worried her lip between her teeth, brows furrowed. "Because boundaries get blurred when you start doing couple-y stuff! Things get...confused."

He couldn't help letting out a guffaw. "I'd say we're long past blurring boundaries. I had my tongue in your—"

"I know!" she yelped. "Which was fine and all—"

"Fine?"

Scarlet splotched her cheeks. "Okay, yes, better than fine. Which is the problem. We—this—well, we might end up doing it again. Then what will we do?"

Waking up with Emma again was really tempting. Minus the overanalytical, freaking-out part.

"You don't want a relationship," she said quietly.

All he could do was nod. There was no denying he didn't commit.

"You don't want to fall in love." Her voice was baffled regret.

His heart twisted. She had it wrong. He had no problem with either of those things. It was the end he didn't want. And he really didn't want to fall short and hurt this woman.

"And we don't share any interests and you think I'm ridiculous to want to dress nice and indulge in shoes and manicures and I'd be better off rolling around in the woods than treating myself to a nice coffee."

"Hey." He rose on an elbow and pinned her with a look. "Now you're putting words in my mouth."

"How? You've been making fun of me for being frivolous since we were kids."

"No more than you've poked at me for being the opposite," he said.

Her disgruntled expression would have been cute were he not feeling like an asshole.

"I'm sorry I insulted you and made you feel ridiculous," he said. "You aren't, not at all. You're... You're sexy. All your bits of glitter and frill. Your legs alone—I could stare at them for days. In trying not to see all those parts of you, I was a dick sometimes."

"Thank you. And...I was no better. I'm sorry, too."

He inched a little closer to her, enough to put his hand on the comforter over what he guessed was her knee.

"You know, as long as we're both aware you aren't interested in a relationship with me, and I'm not looking for anything serious, I don't see why we can't enjoy some—" he lifted an eyebrow "—some extra festivities."

She gave him a dubious look.

"Some things don't need to be planned, Emma. They can just be."

Her dry laugh filled the cabin. "See, you clearly don't know me at all."

"Sure, I do. You probably had some Mr. Right list back in high school—one I wouldn't have lived up to in a million years."

Her eyes went round.

"Wait." He'd been kidding, but the guilt on her face was too real. "Am I right?"

"I was a naïve teenage girl. Sue me." She pulled the comforter tighter around her body.

"You don't still have one, do you?"

She blinked, looking like a deer picking up the scent of a predator.

"I'm kidding, honey, I know you wouldn't—"

"There's nothing wrong with having expectations. I've just always believed the guy for me is out there. And finding someone who shares my interests and goals seems logical." One of her hands poked out from under the covers and she examined her fingers, worrying at the skin of her thumb with the nail of her pointer finger."

"Em…" She wouldn't meet his gaze. He shifted closer yet and covered her hand with his, stilling the nervous motion. "Look, I say this because I respect you, and after we've enjoyed each other a little, you're going to want to keep looking for the one who'll keep you happy for a lifetime. You won't find him if you're comparing your dates to a damn checklist. Whoever told you falling in love was like shopping for a mattress was wrong."

"I don't have a *checklist*." She yanked her hand away. "And no offense, but between my grandmother's advice and yours, I think hers is the more reliable."

Heat crept into his own face. "I'm not entirely without experience. I've fallen in love before."

Her expression softened. "Your fiancée."

"Yeah. And someone in college, though I didn't tell her."

Her mouth fell open.

"What?" He rubbed the back of his neck.

"How could you not pursue someone you were in love with? What if she was the one?"

He flopped back on the pillow. This was not where he'd expected the conversation to go, and it was making his stomach crawl. "She wasn't."

"Who was she?"

"Someone in one of my study groups. She's married to someone else now." And all the better for it.

"Luke—"

"Stop. Please."

She sighed. "Fine. I need to get ready for dinner at my parents' tonight. Sunday tradition."

Man, that sounded nice. Having a big family around the table, shooting the breeze and giving each other the gears. He loved Gramps, but it made for a small crowd, even when Brody came to visit. And with his mom staying in Colorado for Christmas with his stepdad and half siblings, the turkey was going to be mighty small this year.

"Will your parents have something special planned given your siblings are in town?" he asked.

"Oh, probably," she said. "The red carpet gets rolled out whenever Bea or Jack returns. And with Bea's engagement…" She groaned.

"I'd offer to come as moral support, but if you classify a private nap as 'couple-y,' then you bringing me to dinner would definitely—"

"That's a great idea."

"It is?"

"Yeah. Everyone's going to be so blinded by Bea's diamond they won't think twice about you being there. And having a guest who's there for *me*, even if only in a friendly capacity, would be nice for a change."

He wasn't going to bother to point out they'd gone way past friendly. She'd been in the room when he'd draped her legs over his shoulders and made her cry out his name. She knew the truth.

And around her family, he'd pretend he hadn't seen her naked.

"Sounds great. Who's driving?"

Chapter Ten

"I can't believe you brought the game warden to dinner. Since when is hot 'n' brawny your thing?" Bea's face lit with mischief as she sipped her wine. She'd pulled Emma from the kitchen into the relative quiet of the living room. The sprawling farmhouse was bright, whites and pale blues and comfortably decorated. No-nonsense like their mother, who was usually too busy with the ranch to fuss with throw pillows and color palettes. A lot of the decor in the main rooms was leftover from when Emma had lived at home and had loved nothing better than to take care of the small details that tied a space together.

"We've been working together this week. He's our neighbor. I was being neighborly," Emma said through her teeth.

Maybe inviting Luke along had been foolish. A decision made in a post-sex haze where she misjudged how family would draw the wrong conclusions. The naked yearning in his eyes when she'd talked about eating with her family had tugged hard on her sympathy strings. And it wasn't like the Halloran table was exclusive. Her siblings frequently brought friends along. Gray had a firefighter pal with him tonight, in fact.

"Neighborly," Bea said. "Likely story. I saw how you were looking at each other during trivia."

"Like he drives me around the bend?"

"Not enough to stop you from inviting him for dinner, though."

Not enough that I stopped myself from inviting him into my bed, either.

Bea sat on the wood floor next to the Christmas tree and pawed through the wrapped gifts, checking the names written on the tags.

"Bea, God, a little tact with the presents," Emma said, leaning against the side of the upright piano. "What would the Seattle society matrons say?"

Bea rolled her eyes. "Just because I'm marrying someone who runs in corporate circles doesn't mean I'm going to become an intrinsic part of them."

"You don't have to live in each other's pockets, but you should have some common ground," Emma said.

"We do," Bea's fiancé said from the arch separating the living and dining rooms. He looked the same as he had the one other time Emma had met him, on a weekend trip to Seattle when he'd spent most of her two days in town at his office. Dirty blond hair, an "I make deals on the golf course" tan and a wardrobe better suited to some snooty private club.

Calling him the white bread of men was an insult to carbohydrates. Not much was better than ripping open a freshly baked French loaf and slathering it in butter, but there were a lot better options than Jason.

Why Bea lit up whenever he came in the room, Emma didn't know, but really, who was she to criticize? She hadn't done much better with her choices.

You're not going to find him if you're comparing your dates to a damn checklist.

Was Luke right? Did she need to let go, be open to finding someone different from the man she'd always envisioned, like Bea had done?

"I plan to be a big help in getting Bea's little shop off the ground," Jason said, taking a seat on the couch and watching Bea rifle around the back of the tree with a fond look in his eye.

"*Little* shop?" Emma exclaimed. She didn't know Jason well enough to call him out more strongly for diminishing her sister's plans.

Bea poked her head over the arm of the couch. "We can't all be planning to run a big-ass fishing lodge, Emma."

"Not what I meant. I was trying to defend you. Starting any business is a huge undertaking, and a florist's shop is no different—"

"You don't think I can handle the responsibility," Bea said.

"I didn't say that," Emma said. "But if you want

me to look over your business plan, make sure it doesn't turn into another ice-cream truck situation, I can."

Pink mottled her sister's cheeks. "See? *But*. No one in this family believes I can stick with anything." She leaned against Jason's knee and frowned. If Jason made the connection he was included in the Halloran family category of "Things Beatrix will eventually leave in the dust," he didn't let on. It wasn't only Bea's failed ice-cream truck; it also was her stint as a theme-park princess and her year working in Costa Rica at a yoga retreat and the dozen other jobs she'd held since dropping out of college.

And it's Bea's life to live, not mine.

Also, despite her sister's patchwork-quilt résumé, she did seem satisfied with her place in a way Emma envied. Maybe there was something to not sweating the small stuff…

"You're great with flowers," Emma said. "I'm sure you'll figure out the business part."

"Your confidence is overwhelming," Bea snarked.

"Well, you don't even know what I'm aiming to do when I buy the lodge, so we're square!"

A hand squeezed her shoulder. A big masculine hand, attached to a big masculine arm encased in the most huggable-looking sweater on the planet. And a hell of a smile. The little hitch on the side, just for her, reminding her of how good a time they'd had in bed today.

Promising he'd double their fun the next time.

He kept his distance, though, and took a sip of

rum and eggnog. "Glad you're driving. Your dad has a heavy hand with the Bacardi."

"I should have warned you." She stole the glass from him and took a sip. "Should have warned you it wasn't Sunday dinner without at least three separate sibling arguments, too."

"Yeah, I caught on to that a few minutes ago. Jack had to get in between Gray and Nora. Nora was going off about some sort of land offer, and Gray was defending the Brooks Flores family, which didn't really make sense, because aren't Nora and Aleja best friends or something? I dunno. All seemed convoluted. Definitely livelier than a night in with Grandpa."

Emma shook her head at his recount. "Nora loves Aleja but can't stand her brother. It's a long story."

Bea snorted. "Nora and Rafe should really get over themselves and jump each other's bones."

"That's not always the solution," Emma scolded.

"Oh, really?" Bea's gaze flicked between Emma and Luke. "I would have thought—"

"Please don't." Panic bubbled at the back of Emma's throat. What had Bea figured out? She could feel Luke stiffening at her side, even with the foot of space between them.

Emma's mom, Georgie, came into the room, wearing an apron over her simple blouse and jeans. Her dark hair, sprinkled with gray, was pulled into a ponytail. "Luke, sweetie, I hope my squabbling children didn't run you out of the kitchen."

"No, ma'am," he said. "I was thinking how there's

nothing like being around family at the holidays. If Grandpa does decide to retire, maybe he and I will head somewhere warm next year. We've never had the chance, and if the festival gets cancelled, it'll likely be easier for him to be somewhere else."

Emma's heart twisted. "I told you, I could figure out a way to spread out the days so most of the events could still take place."

He squeezed her shoulder again, a look of warning in his eyes. He clearly didn't want to have that conversation right now.

Her mom didn't get the memo. "I didn't realize you'd put so much thought into buying the place."

I've only been talking about it for years.

"I have a full business plan, Mom, and Uncle Edward's commitment to guarantee my mortgage and to lend me whatever my mortgage and savings don't cover. Transforming it back to how Grammy and Gramps had it. But better. I could have renovations on the lodge completed by the end of the summer and be hosting weddings come fall."

Luke spluttered middrink and coughed into his elbow.

Georgie lifted her dark brows. "You okay?"

"Yeah," he croaked. "Went down the wrong pipe."

"The eggnog, or my daughter wanting to renovate the lodge?"

Nerves fisted around Emma's throat. "Mom."

He blinked. "Uh, little of both?"

"I'm not the only person who will put in an offer with the intention of changing some things," she said.

"Fishing to weddings is more than 'some things,' Em," her mom said.

"It's not just a fishing lodge. It's a wilderness lodge. And whose side are you on here?"

"It's a big investment," her mom said evenly. "Even with my brother's help."

"I know," she said. "And it's for Hank, Luke and me to discuss."

"All right, then," Georgie said. "Anyway, dinner's up."

They made their way into the dining room.

Luke bent his head to hers. "So it's not just a fishing lodge?"

"Oh, shush."

"I figured your parents would be contributing to your cash flow."

She shook her head. "The ranch takes everything they have. Hence asking my uncle to back me—he has more liquid assets." And thankfully, Uncle Edward liked her ideas, too, even though it would mean her not working for him anymore.

Both table leaves were in tonight to account for the crowd. Delicious smells wafted off family-style platters of flank steak and roasted vegetables. She and Luke took seats next to each other at her dad's end of the table, across from Bea and Jason. Nora was already digging into the mashed potatoes. Gray and his work buddy were at the other end of the table, talking in awed voices with Jack about something fire related. Whenever Jack made the trip from his smoke-jumping base in Oregon, it inevitably turned into hero-worship central with Gray and his fire-fighting friends.

She cocked her head at Luke. "When you worked with Jack, was it smoke-jumping?"

"Nope. I'm not one for planes. I was on the land crew."

"Mmm," she murmured. "Still super sexy."

Amusement flashed across his face. "Never would have thought of it as your thing."

Me, neither.

It had nothing to do with the firefighting, and everything to do with how Luke doing *anything* would be sexy.

Emma's mom led a quick grace and then started off the feast, scooping carrots and parsnips onto her plate. "Okay, weekly roundup! I'd say Bea and Jason win the prize, for getting me exponentially closer to having grandbabies."

"Mom," Bea said. "One step at a time."

"Tick tock," Emma whispered to Luke.

"Tick tock!" Georgie said.

The conversation turned to Jack, who had far more to recount about his life since he hadn't been for a visit in a few months.

"When are you giving Paisley a ring, sweetie?" Georgie said.

"Why do you think I'm flying back on Christmas Day?" he grumbled.

Congratulations and happy yelps flew around the table, and a flurry of discussion about how Jack was going to propose, and how Jason had proposed, and if either couple had any plans for where a ceremony would take place.

Hmm, maybe all the diamond rings could have a side benefit—

"One or both of you will have to get married at the lodge once I buy it and renovate it," Emma said. "I'd make it perfect for you."

Everyone at the table swiveled in her direction, even Gray's friend. The combined stares made the back of her neck crawl. Jeez. She couldn't tell what everyone was thinking. That she was trying to steal the spotlight from both Bea's and Jack's news? Or that they thought her business plan was a silly idea?

Only Luke was looking at her with a thoughtful expression instead of a critical one.

"Not to distract from all the diamonds," she said. "It would just be fun to hold a family wedding at the same place Grammy and Gramps got married."

Bea's expression softened. "You'd have to buy the place, first. Have you started the process?"

"Well, if we're into the nonwedding part of the roundup," Nora interjected, "I'm still pissed Aleja and I weren't able to win the triple crown this year with her not feeling well. And her brother decided to be a total dick by emailing and offering to buy the east pasture and a quarter of our cattle. *Again.*"

Only the presence of guests held Emma back from whipping a dinner roll at her older sister's head. *Seriously?* "Nora, Bea asked me a question."

"And it's moot, because you're clearly not getting anywhere with the purchase." Nora shook her head in the superior-older-sister way she'd been perfecting since Emma was born. "Even with this whole 'volunteer for the holidays' gambit."

Luke paused with his fork halfway to his mouth. "I wouldn't call it a gambit. Emma's been invaluable this week."

Her chest warmed, and she glanced at his handsome face to check for signs he was being disingenuous. He appeared to be serious. Earnest, almost.

Earning his dinner, for sure.

She dropped her hand to her side and gave his thigh a quick squeeze of thanks.

He covered her hand with his.

Okay, then. Holding hands under the table was *on* the table. Good thing everyone else was too busy stuffing their faces and looking at Bea's honking engagement ring to notice.

"It's a waste of time," Nora said. "As if Hank is going to sell to someone who wants to renovate and hold weddings."

"He intends to at least listen," Luke said. "Emma has a solid business plan, and she's passionate about your family's connection to the property."

"We have *this* family property to care about first," Nora said.

Emma's fork skidded across her plate with a screech. "And my plans wouldn't interfere with the ranch. Which you'd know, if you'd bothered to pay attention."

The table went quiet.

Emma's stomach twisted. Crap. She hadn't meant

to sound petulant. She forced a smile. "Maybe another time, I could show you," she said. "So, what's so offensive about Rafe's offer?"

Nora launched into a long-winded explanation. At least it got the focus off Emma. For once, she didn't want to be the topic of conversation.

She ate the rest of her dinner with one hand, expecting Luke to unwind their fingers.

He didn't, not until it was time to clear the table.

"Are we sticking around long?" he said, voice low. "I have plans for you later."

She winked at him. "You know how I feel about plans."

Luke's "plans" involved cutting out ASAP and getting Emma back to the cabin so he could take her mind off everything that had made her frown during dinner.

An hour after finally extracting themselves from the train-travel game Bea and Nora had insisted on playing, he had Emma naked, rosy cheeked and blissed out. He hadn't minded teaming up with her for the game, especially since they'd won. For all he needed to use strategies to read and write, he was good at maps. Together they'd been unbeatable.

But seeing her post-victory grin was nothing compared to having her smile against his bare chest now. He could get addicted to making her moan and whimper and cry out his name.

Gathering her up, he stroked her back and side with a lazy hand. "Feel better?"

"Mmm, mostly. I might want to do it again."

He chuckled. "Give me a minute. Or twenty."

She stacked her hands on his chest and propped her chin on them. "Thanks for defending me tonight. Even if you had to lie."

"I didn't lie."

One dark brow arched high. "'Emma has a solid business plan'?"

"It's true."

Her mouth pursed. Ah, yeah, there it was—all he needed to get hard again.

"I ever tell you how hot you are with sex hair and your mouth freshly kissed?"

"I don't believe you have." Her eyes sparkled. "The swim this morning feels like it was a month ago."

He tucked a loose strand of hair behind her ear. "I'm glad time slowed down once you started taking my clothes off."

"For you, too?"

"I'm not sure. I think I'll need a bigger sample size," he said. "Do you want me to head over to my own side of the cabin?"

She slowly shook her head.

Anticipation shimmied in his veins. "And we have an easy day tomorrow, too. Only the ice cream buffet after dinner—the kitchen staff will take care of most of that."

"An actual day off?"

"Yeah. Supposed to get above thirty, too—I'm

going fishing," he said. Quiet time, just him, trying
to land a fly in the precise spot on the rushing water.

A hand traced across his chest and toward his
abs. Hmm. Maybe tomorrow needed to be spent *in-side* the cabin.

No. He couldn't pass up a sunny day, not even for
the promise of those fingers.

"I've been so busy with the festival, my fishing
rod's feeling neglected," he said.

Her palm slipped lower. "Oh, I think your rod's
doing fine for himself."

A bark of laughter escaped him. "Corniest joke
of the day, Em."

She smiled. "You still laughed."

"Come with me. I'll show you the best place to
snag a beauty trout."

Recognition flared on her face.

Wait. No. He hadn't meant to quote himself. When
she'd rejected him after he'd said those words to her
the last time, he'd sworn never to repeat them. Way
to remind her of their past awkwardness *and* give
up his alone time on the river.

"Never mind," he said quickly. This was only supposed to be a few days of fun together. Fishing didn't
fit into casual sex.

She cupped his cheek. "You remember asking me
that? Down to the actual words?"

He jerked a nod. Words and he didn't always get
along, but those ones—and her rejection—had stuck.

"I don't regret saying no," she said. "I was still
hurting from getting dumped, and you would have

done the same when you left for Oregon. Going to the river with you would have been an exercise in teenage foolishness."

He winced. "Foolishness. Right. And it's no different, now. I get it. Unless it happens in a bed, you're not—"

"No. It's not the same." A genuine smile lit up her face, stealing his breath. "Take me fishing, Luke. I know you won't let me regret saying yes."

"Brown is not my color."

"Huh?" Luke looked up from the rod and reel he was prepping for Emma to use.

The lodge's equipment and tackle room, usually one of his happy places, seemed strangely charged with her in it.

The odd energy hummed along his skin. Why, he didn't know. It was after eleven, and the sun shone through the windows at the front of the space, promising good times on the river.

Emma stood between two racks, one for life vests and one of rods for rent. She planted her hands on her hips and sent Luke a bemused look.

She was bundled from head to toe in fishing apparel borrowed from the lodge's collection—a waterproof jacket under her brown chest waders, and a small life vest. Her only nod to her usual style was the white knit cap tugged over her forehead and ears. Two long braids stuck out the bottom, one draped over each of her shoulders.

He let out an exaggerated groan. "I thought you were beautiful naked, but in chest waders…"

"Lies," she grumbled.

He put down the rod and went over to adjust her suspenders. With her mouth right there, plump and glossy, he couldn't not give her a little kiss.

Well, maybe not little.

He deepened the caress, cupping the back of her head and losing himself in the taste of mint tea and Emma.

Her gasped breath warmed his lips. "Not sure I'll need those hand warmers you had me put in the toes of my boots anymore."

"I promised you wouldn't get too cold," he said.

"You promised me a good time. So far, my toes are warm and my mouth is tingling, but I'm still not convinced about fishing."

Luke held in a chuckle. There had to be a reason why she'd agreed to join him. And he'd figure it out. He already knew it wasn't the fashion. "Give me a couple of hours. I'll make it worth your while."

She'd enjoy herself if it damn well killed him. There was no better way to fall in love with fishing than to get out there and do it.

He went back to prepping the rod and reel, and to checking his flies. "We're going to use nymphs today. They hatch year-round, so if we catch it right, we could lure in some unsuspecting trout—"

She clearly wasn't paying attention. She was wandering around the front of the room, studying the windows and the outside door connecting the lodge to the network of river trails.

"You brought your license, right?" he said, gathering up their supplies.

"Hmm?" She looked up from where she was studying the rubber flooring. "Oh, yeah. You don't get to arrest me today."

"Ticket you," he corrected.

"Sorry to ruin your fun."

"This is the opposite," he said. "We're going to *have* fun."

She mumbled something about a facial and massages.

"I missed that," he said.

Her cheeks pinkened. "I said, this would be way more fun if it involved a massage."

"Be good, and I'll give you one later."

But he'd lost her again. She was holding her fingers up like a photographer did when they were framing, squinting through the rudimentary square. *"Luke."*

Her "I have a brilliant idea" tone was a warning shot through his belly.

He lifted a brow at her. "Yeah?"

"All this natural light? This room would make an *amazing* spa." She waved a hand toward the windows. "Super multipurpose. A small yoga class for a wedding party or a group of family or friends. Couples or group massages, pedicures and manicures for a bride and bridesmaids—"

His ears buzzed, drowning out whatever else she

was going on about. How the hell could she get from racks of fishing equipment to wedding parties swilling champagne and picking nail polish colors?

He couldn't stop himself from laughing.

She crossed her arms. *"What?"*

"You're not turning the tackle room into a spa."

She snatched her rod off the table and stomped toward the door. "One of these days, you're going to see my vision, Luke Emerson."

Twenty minutes later, she stood an arm's length to Luke's right, hip deep in the river, shoulders rigid as she fought the rod and the line. He hadn't bothered to bring his own rod into the water with them—two lines would guaranteed end up tangled.

"You need to relax, honey. Remember on the front cast, your rod's a pencil and you're drawing a straight line in front of you with the tip."

She'd done okay when they practiced in a nearby clearing with a piece of yarn instead of a hook, but she'd tensed up the second they waded into the river.

"I *am* relaxed," she said, jaw clenched tighter than the set of pliers he had in his pocket to get a fish off a hook.

"You're wound a little tight. The secret's in the wrist."

"Guys always say that."

"Mind out of the gutter, Em. Watch me. It's two movements." He borrowed her rod and showed her the overhand cast again. "Back cast, front cast. Back to ten o'clock, let it fully extend—" he waited until his line was at the apex "—and then forward. No figure eight, or there won't be enough weight in your line." His line sailed over the deep, slow-moving pool. He repeated the motion a few times.

Her brows were tense, dark brown slashes between her Hollywood-starlet sunglasses and the ribbed edge of her hat. "Okay. One more try." She brought her line back like he'd described.

"Yes, and forward now," he said.

"Extend," she echoed. "In the wrist."

"No, not—"

Her line zipped in his direction.

He ducked. His hat lifted from his head. Cold air blew through his hair. "What the—"

"I am so sorry!" Emma gripped her rod in one fingerless-gloved hand and covered her mouth with the other.

His winter fishing hat, the one with earflaps, bobbed about twenty feet downstream, moving with the current.

"Reel it in," he said.

"It's… I don't think it's still hooked."

He sighed. "It happens."

"Was it a lucky hat?"

As if he would go fishing in anything less than a lucky hat. "Had some good flies on it, but I can make more."

Her face crumpled. "I am terrible at this."

"Hey. You're learning." He closed the distance between them, and almost slipped on his ass. Not from the slick rocks. From Emma in her mismatched getup, face sunlit and flushed, water swirling around her legs.

He unzipped his phone from the waterproof pocket by his chest and took a picture.

"What are you doing?"

"You need a memento of the day you caught your first fish," he said.

"But I haven't—"

"You will."

He nestled her against his front. Damn, holding her felt right. The layers of waterproof material between them didn't matter. Her sweetly curved ass was still perfection.

And his chest waders were normally way looser in the crotch.

Sure this is a good idea?

Yes. He'd get her a fish if it was the last thing he did.

Chapter Eleven

Water burbled around Luke, the only soundtrack aside from Emma's frustrated muttering. He shifted her in front of him, putting his hands over hers. She was the perfect height to fit against him—tall enough he wasn't going to get a crick in his back. Soaking in her sweet scent, he guided her movements, erasing the problematic hitch.

"Let's up our game a bit," he murmured in her ear, getting their left hands in play with feeding the line, adding a bit of flair with the rod. "Watch your back cast all the way."

She followed instructions but looked preoccupied. "I feel so bad I lost your hat."

"Forget about it. Eyes on your line." Back. Front. Back. Front. Their jackets rasped together, the casting motion imprinted on his muscle memory since before he started shaving. Though, soon after he'd started shaving, he'd started messing around with girls, and well… The rhythm was kind of the same.

"You take over," he said, voice rasping. He held her hips, letting her control the rod and line, trying to minimize the way her body was rubbing against his, making him hard as the river rocks under his boots.

"I—I've got it!"

"You do." He smiled, kissing her earlobe. "You're doing great."

"I bet you tell that to all the women you take fishing."

"I haven't taken a woman fishing since Cara."

She paused in her movement. The fly sank under the current. She turned her head to look at him. The round disbelief in her eyes was barely visible through the dark lenses of her sunglasses.

"How?" she said.

"Not something I do with a woman I'm casual about." *Until today.*

Her lips parted, a kissable pink O.

"Usually," he corrected.

"Right."

She turned back to the river. "Shoot, where'd my line go?"

"Reel it in and reset," he said.

She leaned against him. The reel clicked and whirred.

The tip tugged.

"Shoot, might have hooked bottom," he said. *There goes another fly...*

The rod flexed again.

"Or it's a fish," she said.

He grinned. "It is."

"Eek, I don't want to fall in."

"I gotcha," he said, gripping her hips.

Her musical laugh tripped along the water. His heart tripped in his chest. There was nothing like a whirring reel, a happy woman and the promise of a great catch.

She reeled like she had a million-dollar fish on the line. "Oh, my God, this is the best."

He caught a flash of brown and silver under the water. "Holy crap, you snagged a good one!"

"How can you see it?"

"Polarized lenses." He took her sunglasses off and put his on her, and then jammed hers on his face because eye protection around fishhooks mattered way more than her glittery sunglasses being a bit small and nowhere near his usual style.

"Oh, my goodness, look at it!"

"It's a beauty. You'll get a few meals out of it if you want."

She looked at him, mouth twisted in horror. "Eat it? *How?*"

"Pan-fried in lemon and butter, usually." She was obviously talking ethics, not cooking techniques, but teasing her was irresistible.

"I can't kill her. She needs to go back into the depths and make all sorts of fishy babies. It's ridiculous, I know—I eat beef and pork and chickens raised by my family all the time. Apparently in the wild, I can't."

"It's not ridiculous." He brushed a kiss on her cheek. "Conservation's critical to the health of the river. The lodge encourages catch and release."

Her luminous grin filled him to bursting. This was exactly what he'd wanted her to see—the joy of the catch. The work the lodge did to help people connect with the river and to protect the ecosystem.

She finished reeling in the fish and she took her gloves off to hold her catch as Luke unhooked it. He snapped a picture of her with her prize.

"Gentle as you release it," he said.

Smiling radiantly, she returned the trout to its chilly home. "That was amazing."

You're amazing. His tongue refused to release the words.

She linked her fingers—her freezing icicles, more like it—behind his neck and kissed him until the chattering river muted and he was lost in a cloud of citrus and fresh air off her skin.

When she finally pulled away, she looked as dazed as he felt.

"I need a picture of us," she said, holding her phone for a selfie.

"With our swapped sunglasses?"

"It's part of the memory."

The memory.

Yeah. He wanted to hang on to this one. Once they were moving on to different things, once he'd

made sure his grandfather turned down—gently—
her purchase offer for good, he would still want to
remember this moment.

Emma gritted her teeth and changed positions on
the front balcony of the lodge where she was taking
engagement photographs for her sister and Jason.
The colors of the trees and lake made for a gorgeous
background, especially with the sun on the rustic
wood railing. Her subjects were the ones being dif-
ficult.

"Bea, peek up at Jason a bit. Work the eye contact. Arms around his shoulders." She moved them
around, getting the angles exactly right. "Seriously,
soften up the faces."

Bea's smile looked doubly stiff through the lens
of Emma's Nikon. She snapped a few shots anyway.

"You know, we didn't ask you for engagement pictures." Bea dropped her arms and glared at Emma.
"This is for you, not us."

"It's for you, too. You need some romantic pictures. You could use them for your save-the-date
cards."

"And you want to be able to use them to prove
some weird point to Luke."

"It's not weird," Emma said. "He needs to see how
romantic this place can be." She pointed across the
balcony. "Try over there next."

The couple was no more relaxed leaning into the
corner of the railing, with Bea's back to Jason's front
and him kissing Bea's cheek.

"Almost there," Emma said. "You just need to—" *to actually look at each other like you're in love* "—to turn on the smolder."

Jason's yacht-club face crinkled with intensity. Constipated intensity.

Emma held in a sigh and captured a few more images.

A flash of tan canvas and buffalo plaid caught her eye at the bottom of the curved stairs. Luke strode along the path, snow shovel in hand. If only Jason could stare at a woman with as much heat as Luke…

An idea popped into her head.

She poked her head over the railing. "Luke!"

He peered up at her, shading his eyes to the midday sun. "Yeah?"

"Are you done with the shoveling?" Emma's impromptu ninth-day activity was tonight, the *Nutcracker* film in the dining room at eight o'clock, leaving them free to do other resort tasks all day. Luke had peeled himself out of her bed early this morning to help the grounds crew.

He'd seemed like he regretted having to leave her.

Maybe they'd have time for another afternoon nap…

"I was going to break for lunch," Luke said.

"I need a favor. Come up here?"

Bea and Jason traded a look.

"Trust me," Emma said.

Heavy steps echoed up the stairs. Luke paused at the top, his gaze beleaguered. "Kinda wanted to take a shower, Em."

"I need you for a second. To show Jason and Bea what I'm getting at with their engagement photos."

She put her camera down and waved Bea and her husband-to-be to the side. "Luke, stand where Jason was. We'll show them the pose I'm aiming for."

"Okay." He sounded doubtful but followed instructions, leaning his elbows on the railing. His jacket parted, exposing the open flannel shirt and black fitted T-shirt he had on underneath.

Her breath caught. To be that cotton, hugging those taut muscles...

He cocked a brow at her.

Right. She closed her gaping mouth and joined him at the railing. Leaning against him, she glanced up and over her shoulder. The scent of work-warmed cotton and fresh air swamped her. His hands went to her hips, and his eyes darkened. Yeah, that's what she'd been going for.

A shutter clicked.

"There," Bea snapped. "Now you have your picture. Can we go?"

"Oh. I didn't mean for you to—actually, never mind. One more," Emma croaked. "Luke, kiss my cheek."

"Oh, good grief." His complaint hummed along her skin as his lips brushed her temple.

His beard rasped her skin. Heat pooled in her belly.

Two more clicks.

Bea's toe tapped a staccato rhythm on the wood planks. "Are we *done*?"

Not nearly.

But what Emma and Luke had to finish wasn't going to happen on the deck of the lodge.

She broke apart from him and accepted her camera from her sister. "You don't want to try a different location? By the river?"

"We're fine with what you got," Jason said. "We're heading into town for lunch."

Emma's heart sank. "I'm sorry I wasn't able to make it magical for you."

Bea lifted a shoulder. "Magic isn't our thing, Em. Don't worry about it."

Don't worry? How could she not?

Her sister and Jason disappeared down the steps.

Her throat threatened to close. If she couldn't even manage to run a flawless photo session, did she have any business taking on bigger events?

"What's wrong?" Luke said.

"The session flopped. And I can't decide if it was because of them, or me."

"I wouldn't panic over your sister and her fiancé not being into pictures." His expression turned dubious. "I'm not sure they're even into each other."

Something she should be more concerned about than business, but Bea got so touchy about her independence. Emma was used to not interfering in her sister's life. She could only find solutions for her own problems.

Was she not suited to the dream she'd had for what felt like forever?

She was still stewing about it during the post-dinner movie. The serving staff had cleared the tables to the side, and lodge guests and Sutter Creek folks were sitting on blankets and camp chairs. The *Nutcracker* ballet danced across a large white sheet hanging in front of the rock fireplace.

Everyone was eating snacks and loving life, except Emma. Well, Luke might not have been, either. He was off tromping through the woods somewhere, having been called in as backup in some sort of emergency.

She buzzed around the dining room, straightening the red cups full of pretzels drizzled with white chocolate and sprinkled with candy cane crumbles. She'd set out plastic shot glasses of red-and-green jelly beans, too. The big tray of sugar cookies was almost empty. So the treats were a hit.

She leaned against one of the wooden support posts under the loft, scanning the crowd to make sure everyone had smiles on their faces. It was almost like the pictures she'd seen of the '70s when her grandparents would haul out an actual film projector and half of Sutter Creek would show up for yet another showing of one of the two movies they'd spent a fortune to buy. Families enjoying themselves, eating too many chips and the kids getting hopped up on soda. This would be another kind of event she could offer to wedding parties if they were looking to make it more of a weekend or weeklong event. A change from Hank's focus.

This is more about you than us.

Bea's earlier accusation made the back of Emma's throat burn. Was she being too selfish with this?

No. Keeping the wilderness focus was no more or less valid than weddings and romance.

Grabbing three jelly bean cups, she tossed a handful into her mouth and chewed, then almost gagged. Right. Cherry and mint looked festive together but didn't work by the handful. She swallowed the poorly flavored lump.

An elbow nudged her. Luke's? Her heart leaped and she turned her head.

"Oh. Hey, Brody."

Amusement crossed his handsome face. "Why the frown? Wrong Emerson cousin?"

"Of course not." She popped a green jelly bean between her lips. "Luke's working."

"Yeah, he does that. All the time."

She shrugged. "Tonight wasn't a two-person job." Probably good to have a breather from each other, too. Too much hot emotion had swelled between them during their picture session.

Brody raked a hand through his sun-streaked hair. "You're more the sort for dating a nine-to-five guy."

Collecting three green candies at once, she avoided eye contact. "Who says we're dating?"

"Uh, you took him to family dinner on Sunday."

She lifted her chin. "You've been to family dinner a hundred times."

"Because Bea and I are friends."

"Luke and I can't be friends?"

"Seems a strange time to start." His arms crossed over his chest. It was, objectively, as sizzling hot as Luke's—Brody spent a hell of a lot of time on the water in a scull. Her stomach didn't tingle at the sight of it, though.

Friends. Yeah, no. She and Luke were so beyond friends.

"Are you worried about your cousin, or the lodge?" Maybe Brody didn't like the idea of her buying it, either.

"Bea was in a snit today, complaining about you being laser-focused on your wedding facility plan," he said. "She's pissed how you've barely been home all week and about some failed photo session."

"Oh." The minty beans turned to sand in her mouth. "Right. Their pictures—miscalculation on my part, I guess." Hopefully the whole plan wasn't a miscalculation. Other people loved engagement sessions and thematic weekends and to have every step just so. "And as for the rest of it, it's important I'm here. I have an arrangement with your grandfather and Luke, and—"

"As long as everyone's clear on the motivations in play."

"I'm not hiding anything, Brody." Not about the lodge, anyway. Her burgeoning connection to Luke was best kept to herself. She held out one of the half-full plastic cups. "Jelly bean?"

He wrinkled his nose. "Wouldn't be much of a coach if I ate stuff I've banned from my athletes' diets."

"Sounds miserable," she said.

"Gold medals make up for it." His gaze shifted to over her shoulder, and he smiled. "For most of us in the family, anyway. This guy's happier with gold*finches*."

Luke stopped at Emma's side, thumbs hooked in his utility belt. "We can't all make the Olympics."

And the flash of pain on his face made his regrets river-water clear.

The urge rose to make him feel better, but really, what could she say? She wouldn't be happy having quit the thing she loved, either.

Brody stared at his cousin for a second and then checked his phone. "I'm going to head into town for some Christmas cheer. Don't do anything you'll regret, kids."

"Probably too late there," she said under her breath, watching Brody meander to the exit.

Luke snatched one of her jelly bean cups and tossed them all back. Distaste twisted his face as he chewed. "That's an awful combination."

"Yeah, I made the same mistake earlier."

"Oh?" He leaned in for a kiss. "You just taste like mint."

Heat rushed into her cheeks. Good thing Brody hadn't seen the obvious proof things were way more complicated than she'd let on. "I was working through the green ones."

"Always a plan, with you."

It didn't come off as a slam like some of his pointed comments had earlier in the week.

She cupped his jaw, stroking his beard with her thumb. He smelled like sugar and the forest, and something clean she guessed was his deodorant. "Survived the woods?"

"Well enough."

"Sucks to lose one of your vacation days." She scanned him from head to toe. Damn, he was wearing a lot of sexy layers she could remove for him. "Though any time you want to get all dressed up in your uniform, you feel free."

"Oh, really?"

"Yup. Nice bum, sugarplum." She jerked her head at the makeshift screen. "If we want to keep it thematic and all."

He chuckled. "Even I know that's Clara, not the sugarplum fairy."

"Details."

His lips landed on the top of her head and he backed her against the support post.

"Luke! This is a family event."

"It's dark. No one's looking." Following the curve of her jaw, he nuzzled a line.

"Mmm."

"Better. Not exactly a smile, but I'll take it."

Reaching up, she threaded her fingers into his hair. Soft, thick, asking to be played with. "There are way too many people in this room."

"And here I thought bringing in crowds was the whole point. Prove you know what you're doing." He indicated the room with a lazy hand. His finger trailed along the collar of her slouchy sweater.

One rasp of a fingertip, and she melted against the post. *Argh.* Was she in over her head?

The Nutcracker finale rang over the speakers.

"Stop," she said lightly. "I still need to direct cleanup."

"*I* need to clean up. I feel like I hiked halfway to Wyoming tonight." The corner of his mouth lifted. "And after, you could direct me."

"Leave your cabin door open, and I will."

She let herself in forty minutes later. The room was the mirror image of hers: king-size bed, two chairs in front of the wood-burning fireplace, small table by the window. Without all the decorations she'd been working on recently, though. And with the presence of one sleeping game warden, still wearing boots. His legs hung off the end of the bed as if he'd locked up his weapons, sat down, flopped back and passed out.

Hmm. She could leave him and go back to her room. She could crawl under the covers on the unoccupied side of the bed. Or she could wake him up and shuffle him off to the shower.

Maybe go with him.

Yup. Option three.

Straddling his muscular thighs, she settled onto his lap. Her red velvet high heels fell to the floor.

Luke groaned. His eyes fluttered open. Gray and clear and an arresting mix of sleepiness and need. He rubbed his palms along her thighs. "I'd hoped you'd keep those shoes on."

"Luke from ten days ago would be shocked to hear you say that."

"That guy hadn't had the privilege of waking up to your smile."

Her breath hitched. Slept with, had sex with— she would have expected him to reference either of those things. Not anything to do with something so sweet, almost innocent, as a smile.

She leaned forward, planting a hand on the mattress on either side of his head and kissing him until she coaxed another groan from him. She trailed her mouth down the strong column of his neck and flicked open a button on his shirt. "You're something else, Luke Emerson."

"Yeah? How so?"

For starters, you like romance more than you're willing to admit.

His skin tasted like salt and winter air. She mouthed the notch below his Adam's apple, smiling as he murmured his appreciation. "You're loyal," she said. "To your family, to the county… And even though that loyalty runs at cross-purposes to mine, it's really hot."

She'd believed him the opposite of her perfect man, but parts of him attracted her in ways she'd never even realized could be a draw.

Gentle fingers brushed her hair off her forehead.

She shifted a few inches lower and kept going on his buttons.

His gaze darkened, anticipation riding on sheer want. "I was serious about wanting a shower, first."

"Lead the way."

Luke leaned against the end of the bathtub stall. The cold tile on his shoulder blades, Emma's hot mouth wrapped around his rock-hard erection—it made his head spin. Water flowed through the silky ribbons of hair streaming over her breasts. And the playful smirk in her eyes…

He didn't want to lose control, not in the shower.

"Stop. Too much."

Her hand and mouth fell away. Confusion and hurt splashed across her face. "No good?"

"I want to finish with you."

"This is 'with me.'" She shut off the water and stood, grabbing one of the beige towels off the top of the glass and wrapping it around her shoulders. "I like it, too, you know."

Cupping the back of her head, he said, "It's not inside you, though. I need that right now."

Her pupils flared.

Using her towel, he dried her off, placing a kiss on each rosy spot until he was on his knees.

Damn, she was gorgeous, those long legs and the soft skin of her belly. He leaned in, unable to resist. One tender kiss to her mound. A little tongue down to the bud.

She moaned, gripping his shoulders.

Standing, he lifted her under her bottom.

Hot, damp folds nestled against his aching length and he almost pitched off the cliff.

You have one job, Emerson. Fifteen feet to the bed.

He stepped out of the tub and somehow made it from the bathroom to the bedroom with her clinging to him, legs hugging his hips, mouth nipping at his neck.

Lined up just right. Not ready for bare, but man, he would not say no if they got there one day.

You never get that close, last that long.

True. But with Emma, it was damn tempting. She inspired a man to be better, to do better.

His knees hit the edge of the bed and he ripped the covers back and laid her on the sheets. Lithe, toned limbs on white cotton. Her gaze, threatening to steal his soul.

Nothing in the world seemed more important than making her forget her name and following her into the abyss.

He grabbed a condom and a bottle from the bedside table, opening the lube first and slowly slicking her folds with his fingers.

Her mouth went slack, a dreamy expression. "You bought some?"

Stealing a taste from her open lips, he nodded. "I want this to be exactly what you need."

Hips lifting, she writhed against his palm. He dipped a finger into her wet heat, then another.

A hitched breath, a murmur of impatience—his? Hers?

Who knew? Another minute of her squirming and begging under his hand, and he'd be spilling on the sheets—

"I don't… I don't think this is—" she breathed out a moan "—what you meant by inside."

He circled her clit with his thumb. "I can be patient. I love watching you lose your hold over your world."

She pulled at his torso, clearly trying to get him to shift over her. "Let's do that together."

After putting protection in place, he knelt between her thighs.

She rubbed a finger around her sex, eyes heavy lidded and beckoning him closer.

Bracing on his elbows over her, kissing her and thrusting deep, it was everything good in the world in one flash of a moment.

Nails dug into his shoulders. Her slick walls tightened around his shaft. He pumped as slow as he could. She seemed like she was getting close, arching her head back and meeting his thrusts with frantic hips.

Sweat beaded on his brow. Holding on was so damn worth it and a battle all at once.

A mewling cry had his heat rushing to his core, and everything pulled tight.

He breathed through it. Reaching a hand between them, he thrummed her swollen bud with a thumb until she clasped around him, electrified and needy.

"Luke."

His name tumbling from her lips—it felt like he'd claimed her as his.

Cupping the back of her head, fingers tangling in damp silk, he buried himself in her. Let everything precious swamp him as he let go. Spun into a blazing space of release, tumbling through time. The woman clinging to him was his only anchor.

Chapter Twelve

Luke loved the fog that drifted in after mind-blowing sex. He held Emma close, nuzzling her hairline. The silky strands, usually straightened, were drying wavy and lush after their shower. She draped her legs over him and stroked a hand along his chest. It was impossible not to be as close to her as the laws of physics allowed.

"I hope you're okay with me staying the night," she said. "There's no way I could bring myself to move right now."

"I'd be disappointed if you left."

She stilled, lips parting as if she was on the verge of speaking.

"Something on your mind?"

A silly question. Emma was never not thinking.

It was part of why he liked using his hands and tongue and body to distract her. Those moments where her gaze went soft, he knew he'd narrowed her focus entirely on her senses.

"Just contemplating tomorrow," she said.

Tomorrow. The reminder of the skating event washed away his bliss like a bucket of water. "Did Brody check the ice thickness? Spread water over the skating surface?"

He'd spent hours of his childhood dunking buckets in a drilled hole and splashing water onto the ice to wash away snow and smooth the surface until it froze up, glassy and pristine. A fist wrapped around his throat. He took a few breaths, waiting until the muscles relaxed.

"Brody assured me everything is under control," she said. "Thought you didn't want to be involved…"

"I don't. I'm going to watch football with Grandpa tomorrow."

She stilled. "You could be part of what draws people to the event, you know. Skating with one of Sutter Creek's hockey stars."

Was she *trying* to rip him open? "I'm not a star."

Her brows knit. "You made it to the pros."

"For nine games."

"Doesn't that count?" she said.

Not when you're an Emerson.

He trailed a hand down her back. She shivered.

"You're ignoring my question."

"No, you're naked, so I have the attention span of a gnat," he said. And if she didn't change the sub-

ject, *he'd* be the one leaving the cabin and finding
somewhere else to sleep.

She climbed on top of him. Her sweet center rode
the base of his thickening erection. "Right. I forgot.
Physical feelings, check. Emotional ones, nope."

"You say that like—"

She tilted her hips. Pleasure rushed through him,
shorting out his thoughts.

Get it together. It's just sex.

"Like it's a bad thing," he finished.

"Bad? No. Damaging, though." Her lips punctuated the soft words, landing on his pec and skidding
across his skin.

Damaging. That was life. And then there was
Emma, clinging to the belief in glittery, unrealistic endings.

He fumbled a hand on the bedside table until he
found a condom. He held it out to her. "Ride me."

She plucked the packet from his fingers. "Be honest with me first."

Blood rushed in his ears. "It's that important to
you?"

"Honesty?"

"No, me talking about the past," he said.

"Only if you want to." Her hips coasted along his
length. "But you're hurting. It's obvious."

"You don't need to fix me, Emma."

"Not trying to."

"No one needs to hear about my hockey career
sucking in comparison to Grandpa's."

Had the color of her eyes pried the words from his

chest? He'd always felt safe standing in a river. When she held his gaze with hers, that green reminding him of some of his happiest days, it was easier to spit out some of the kernels he usually kept buried deep.

Plush lips landed on the corner of his mouth. The gentlest of kisses, accepting his truth. "You know you can't live his life, right?"

"You're one to talk." He laughed, dry and rusty. "Your whole plan is about your grandmother."

She frowned. "Inspired by her, sure, but it's my own take. My own dream, not hers."

"And hockey was mine." He wanted to thrust into her, cut off further conversation before it could go somewhere worse. "Put the condom on me, Emma."

"Sure." Gentle fingers sheathed him. She collected a few drops of lube from the bottle and stroked his length from head to hilt.

Gasping, he gripped her thighs. "Thought I told you to ride me."

"I will." She rose, taking the tip of him into her slick, hot sex. A smile hinted at the corners of her mouth. "I went fishing with you, you know."

"I—" He was ready to beg and plead and tell her anything, to get her to sink lower until her warm, wet flesh kissed the base of his erection. She slid down an inch. Spots danced across his vision. "Take me in."

"Mmm." Another inch. "Don't you think if I went fishing, you need to come skating?"

Holy hell, what he needed was oblivion. "You're playing dirty, Halloran."

She sank a little lower.

"In the morning, I'll… I'll make sure the ice is ready," he said. "That's all I can do."

"Okay, Luke."

He should have felt relieved.

But her faltering smile… Damn it.

He flipped her over and drove into her sweet heat, sealing his mouth over her squeal of surprise.

Early the next afternoon, Hank was kicked back in his recliner, and for whatever reason was focused on Luke instead of on the college football bowl game they'd decided to watch. "I appreciate the company, son. Still, I call BS on you wanting to be here instead of out on the ice."

Luke wasn't biting, no matter how hard his grandfather tried to get him to talk. He waved at the TV with more emphasis than a marginal call deserved. "Oh, come on! As if that was a flag."

Emma's cat squawked, digging her claws through Luke's jeans. He hissed in pain and the cat darted off his lap and into Hank's bedroom.

"You worried you've forgotten how to skate?" Hank said lightly.

The question landed on Luke's shoulders like a tree blown over in a storm. He swallowed, resisting the lump threatening to fill his throat. "Did you see that play?"

"Can't say I did."

"Freaking travesty."

Hank coughed.

"Need your inhaler?" Luke asked.

"Nope. I need you to get off your ass and go check on your girl."

"She's not—"

He couldn't get the words out. They weren't quite true anymore. Not after last night. He'd gotten too close to her to pretend they weren't involved.

"So what is she, then?" Hank asked.

Eventual heartbreak. "Who knows?"

"Well, figure it out. She deserves better than to be someone's uncertainty."

Luke's throat went acidic. "She does."

"Then get down to the lake and tell her how you feel," Hank ordered.

Easier to do if he knew how he felt.

"I'm not avoiding Emma. I just don't want to play the glory days game," he grumbled. "You know how people are. You deal with it all the time, people wanting to reminisce."

"Which is a good time."

Not when your glory days ended in a big choke-fest.

"Emma doesn't need me to help out. Not with Brody down there."

"They're not experts, though."

Neither am I.

"Look," Luke said. "I know it's hard for you not to be shooting the breeze with everyone and taking your Bauers out for a spin. I wish I could speed up your healing process. I really do."

"And I feel the same about yours."

Luke's chest hollowed and he stared at his grandfather. "I don't know what you mean."

"You've been mighty clear about not wanting to discuss your hockey career. That's doing you no favors," Hank said.

"I can't change the past."

Hank shook his head. "Grief is a strange animal, son."

"Grief? Huh?" His stomach pulsed, unsettled. What the hell were they talking about, here? Was it something to do with his grandmother? "It makes sense you'd be thinking of Grandma this week. Must be hard not to have her around for the festival. For everything."

Hank served him a long-suffering blink.

"Is that not what you meant?" Luke said.

"You'll figure it out. And you should do some of that figuring down on the ice today. Emma *doesn't* need you to organize anything, but she wants you there. If you hold back, it'll only hurt the both of you."

The crowd noise off the television buzzed in his ears, matching the hum of his thoughts. Like a wasp flying out of range. Not quite visible but close enough to hear, carrying the threat of a sting. The back of his neck prickled.

Holding back would hurt her? In what world? He'd made no promises. She hadn't wanted him to.

Don't you think if I went fishing, you need to come skating?

He rested his head on the back of the couch. Him

getting on the ice after more than a decade wasn't the same as her going into a river. She hadn't been dealing with fear and loss.

Grief.

Wait, was that what Grandpa was on about? He thought Luke needed to grieve what he'd lost: hockey?

The older man's attention was back on the game. A frown darkened his face.

Luke knew he was responsible for it. Emma's disappointment, too. He'd buried her point under a wave of pleasure and sexual distraction last night, but he couldn't avoid it in bright daylight. By not going, he was letting her down.

No surprise there.

So change it.

"I could go see if she needs help," he croaked.

"Yep."

A rush of nerves spread from his core to the tips of his fingers and toes. Opening himself up to questions, to all those sorry looks.

He stood. "I'll go for a few minutes."

"Sure." Hank cleared his throat. "My skates are in the back of the hall closet if you need to borrow them. Might be a half size too big. Wear thick socks."

Encouragement and love infused Hank's gaze. The sort of support he'd always given Luke, despite Luke's lack of follow-through.

Well, this time, Luke could follow through. For Hank *and* for Emma.

"I'll be back in a few." He collected what he

needed. Gloves. Coat. Courage. Worse came to worst and someone was a dick, he could laugh it off like Emma had been doing all week every time she'd ended up facedown in the snow. He snagged the skates, gripping the tied laces in a fist.

"Take your time, son. Nothing prettier than watching a woman glide around a frozen lake in the sunshine."

Ten minutes later, standing outside the semicircle of wooden logs serving as a place for people to sit and lace up, Luke pulled out his phone and texted Hank a picture of the swirl of people on the ice, along with one word: Proof.

Grandpa: Good. And I was right.

Luke sent back a confused-face emoji.

A screenshot of the picture Luke had just taken popped up in the window with a red circle drawn around one of the skaters. Emma, twirling and laughing, wearing a pink puffer jacket, a matching Santa hat and a radiant smile.

Her photograph was enough to make his heart skip a beat. Lifting his head, he braced himself for the effect of the real thing. And for the first time since he'd hung up his skates, his feet itched to put them on. Not because he wanted to join the group of U-15 kids passing the puck around. Because he wanted to hold hands with the Barbie-pink-hatted woman and listen to her blades swish as he spun her around.

Straightening, he settled onto one of the empty tree stumps and unlaced his boots. He left them on the thick canvas covering the ground, spread out to save blades while people wobbled the few feet to the lake.

The whole setup was similar to the swan swim. A few fire barrels for warming hands, apple cider and cocoa with marshmallows on a table. Unlike the events up by the lodge and the river, no music played. The wind snapped in his ears. Snow blew across the ice, a sibilant whisper.

Five minutes. Go out there, show Emma he was willing. Take off before anyone decided to travel down memory lane.

He stepped gingerly from the canvas to the frozen surface.

Pushed off, like he'd done thousands of times going from the bench to the ice. Practices. Games.

Brody raced over to him, stopping abruptly a few feet away. A shower of snow pelted Luke from head to foot.

He brushed off his coat and glared at his cousin. "Thanks, jackass."

"Quite the cobwebs trailing off those skates."

Gritting his teeth, he headed in Emma's direction. "They're Grandpa's."

"I see what drew you down here," Brody said.

"Certainly wasn't your glowing self."

Brody snorted and caught Luke's shoulder, forcing him to stop. "You look good out here."

"I look like a thirty-four-year-old washup who's forgotten how to do more than glide."

Jerking his chin, Brody said, "I don't think she defines you that way."

Luke turned, caught one glimpse of the joy on Emma's face and promptly lost his footing. He landed on his ass with a thud.

Snickering, his cousin leaned down and patted him on the head. "Slick as always."

The scrape of blades faded as Brody returned to the informal kids' game.

Emma finally spotted him. Her mouth rounded in surprise. Cheeks bright from exertion, she glided toward him. "Are you okay?"

Legs spread wide in a steadying stance, she held out her mittened hands in an offer to help him up.

He took both her hands in his and kissed the knitted material somewhere in the vicinity of her knuckles.

"Crafty, Emerson!" a voice called from over by the kids playing pick-up. "You always did like to spend part of a game on your keister. Who knew the ladies liked it?"

Irritation made the hairs on Luke's neck crawl. He scrambled to his feet and sent the minor-league coach a wave instead of the middle finger the guy deserved.

Emma tugged his hands, pulling his attention to her. "You came."

"Grandpa wasn't going to get off my back until I did."

Her expression dimmed, and he realized how he'd sounded.

Leaning in, he nuzzled the plush brim of her hat. "I came for you, honey."

She caught his mouth with hers. A brush of a kiss. He felt it down to his toes.

He lowered his voice. "Any chance your panties match your hat?"

Wicked heat glinted in her eyes. "Want to find out?"

"Hell yes."

"Depends on your pairs skating technique, I guess."

He groaned. "You're a terror."

"I try to be." She smiled, genuine encouragement lighting up her eyes. "Show me what you can do."

"Like riding a bike, right?" Taking her hand, he tugged her in a wide circle, sticking to the outside of the fifteen or so people making up the last group of skaters. Hesitance weighed his muscles as he eased back into the rhythm of crossovers and gliding. Part from lack of practice, part because he didn't want to lose his grip on Emma.

"Faster?" he asked.

"Not me." She let go of his hand. "I want to see *you* fly."

Shooting her a grin, he took off. Every eye on the ice was on him.

It didn't matter. It was about his body falling back into long-rejected patterns. About wind whipping in his ears and the cold on his skin. The shouts from the kids didn't hurt, either.

His chest loosened.

Being out here wasn't comfortable. The knowledge his mental game had never matched his physical pricked as always. But it wasn't the humiliation he thought it would be.

He took another lap, winking at Emma as he looped past her. What if falling in love was the same? If he could somehow figure out a way to have this glowing woman in his life—

Not if I want to keep from hurting her.

He could get out and skate all he wanted. It didn't change the past, how he hadn't managed to follow through on all the effort his coaches and family had put into his career, into the embarrassment of all those headlines.

His blades scraped the ice and he slowed.

"Thought your skating would get you a cup one day, Emerson," the kids' coach said.

"Didn't we all," Luke muttered.

"You had your grandfather's feet. Probably not his hockey sense, though. Total legend."

Luke nodded and forced a smile.

"Luke, heads up!"

He turned. A hockey stick arced in the air, heading way off course from where his cousin intended it to go. He snagged it.

"God, your reflexes." Brody shook his head. "Still epic."

"And your terrible aim." Luke turned the stick in his hands. It felt foreign.

He caught Emma's gaze. She was watching him,

brows knitted in concern. What was he doing here? He didn't need to relive any of this. He'd already failed at continuing his grandfather's excellence on the ice. He couldn't change that. He needed to focus on the now, the lodge, helping his grandfather retire like he wanted and making sure everything he'd built stayed intact.

"Want to play with us, Emerson?" the coach said.

The kids cheered.

"A real NHLer!" one of them shouted.

"For a few games," Luke specified, his gut urging him to retreat. Playing with the kids did not count as a quick five-minute in-and-out. "My grandpa and I used to play out here every Christmas afternoon if the lake was frozen. He always bought me new skates."

He felt Emma's eyes on him, and he cocked his head at her. "Want to join, too, Halloran?"

She shook her head. "You need spectators."

Paparazzi was more accurate. She had her phone up the whole time while he tossed the puck around with the kids.

By the time the guests were gone and Brody was driving the ATV and trailer back to the lodge with all the equipment, it was almost dark.

Emma straightened her hat, rewrapped her scarf and headed for one of the trails. Not one leading directly to the lodge, though.

"Em, you're on the wrong path." He hurried to follow her.

"I'm taking the long way. I think we're close to

the clearing where my grandparents got married, and I want to check it out."

His pulse kicked up. Her grandparents' ceremony wasn't the only wedding held in that clearing. Well, that had been *planned* to take place there.

He didn't feel like facing another ghost of his past today. "It's going to get dark."

Emma's sigh was so loud, he expected it to blow snow off the branches of the nearby evergreens. "I'll use the flashlight app on my phone."

The snow was packed along the trail—it was one of the more popular ones for snowshoeing.

"All right. The long way it is," he said.

"Don't feel obligated if you don't want to come." The staccato words echoed in the empty woods.

"Buddy system."

They trudged for a few minutes and got to a crossroads.

"Head left, honey."

Peering to the right, she came to a halt. "Isn't that it there? I only ever came down here with Grammy in the summer."

"I don't know," he lied. The trees were taller than the day Cara had run through them, escaping in the middle of their rehearsal. Thank God she'd had the sense to recognize marriage would have been a mistake. He'd have made her miserable, wouldn't have been able to give her anywhere near the life she wanted.

"Let's check!" Emma said.

He grimaced. "The trail's not packed down. You'll get snow in your boots."

"What's a little snow in the face of family history?"

It only took one step for snow to trickle into Emma's boots. No matter. The sunset's pink glow colored the white carpeting the clearing, luring her forward. The trees opened into a space large enough for a forty-foot-long aisle, and wide enough to have ten chairs on each side. At the end, covered in snow, an arch of some sort cast a long shadow.

"Luke, is that…?" Ignoring the cold seeping into her socks, she tromped toward what had to be a human-made structure. "It's an *arbor*?"

"Emma." Pain turned her name into a plea.

She spun to face him about five feet from the wooden arch. "What?"

His expression was as hard as the icy lake in the distance. "Can we go?"

"Look at this!" She swept an arm from the forest to the view of the lake and the sunset slowly turning to lavender. "I know you think my ideas are silly, and they don't fit with what you love about the lodge. It's wonderful for all it does for outdoorspeople. It could also be wonderful for people who want to get married. Could you think of a place more beautiful than this?"

She clearly wasn't going to get a response from those thin-pressed lips. She went over to the arbor and brushed some of the snow from the frame. The wood looked worn.

"Do you know who had a ceremony here?" she said. "Someone must have. This is handmade."

He crossed his arms. "No one got married here."

"But—"

"I built the arbor."

She froze. Intense cold filtered through her socks, shooting through her anklebones. "For when—"

He looked like if he moved, even so much as to speak, he'd shatter.

"Your fiancée left you that close to the wedding?"

"Yeah. While we were holding the rehearsal. There." He pointed to the spot right behind Emma.

"Luke…" Tears pricked her eyes. Getting left at the altar was no small thing. And yet, she was puzzled, too. It seemed like something a person could move on from—eventually, anyway.

He stacked his hands on his beanie-covered head, staring at the archway.

Realization filtered in. "Hang on, is that part of why you're opposing my plan? You weren't able to get married at the lodge, so no one can?"

Heat turned his eyes a molten gray. "What the hell are you talking about?"

"Your whole 'my grandfather's legacy' song and dance. Are you sure it isn't more to do with the wedding angle? It's too painful for you to face how your fiancée abandoned you, and what I'm proposing to build will bring it all back?"

"Song and dance?" His posture was rigid, stiff as the arbor he'd carefully crafted.

She lifted her chin. Her accusation was harsh, sure. But she had to know.

"Why don't you pick apart your own coping mechanisms instead of poking at mine?"

"Like what?"

"Uh, selective listening? Because there's no way someone who was married for fifty years would have told you a relationship would always feel like standing in a ray of freaking sunshine."

The verbal slap landed hard. She shivered. From the cold in her feet and legs, sure.

From the truth.

She got in her own way when it came to relationships. Clinging to the letter of her grandmother's advice rather than seeing the kernels of wisdom. The man in front of her provided all sorts of proof there was good to be found, connections to be made, even if differences and imperfections existed.

"You're—" She swallowed. "You're right."

He blinked, clearly surprised.

"I *should* work on that. I *will*, I mean." She took a step toward him and curved her mittened hand around his forearm. "If I work on accepting a relationship will have flaws, and that the man for me might be nothing like what I've always pictured, would you be willing to meet me halfway?"

He caressed her cheek. "We didn't agree to a relationship."

"I know. And you're still hurting at the mere sight

of something you built over a decade ago, which tells me there's probably more going on."

"Would you stop, already?" Close-to-breaking pain flickered across his face again.

She didn't want to stop. Her feelings for him were shifting and growing, and she wanted to explore them. But she wasn't about to enter something one-sided. She glanced out at the lake, now fully blanketed by the darkened sky. "I should get back to my cabin. I'm going to lose a toe if I'm not careful."

The journey up the trail was quiet, suffocating. He disappeared into his side of the cabin without a word.

Chapter Thirteen

Pictures blurred on Emma's laptop screen as she scrolled through the shots she'd captured since the first day of the festival. She had lots of wedding-related pictures to take and use in her proposal. The memory shots stood out the most. Her Brownies and their tree. Family and friends making happy fools of themselves with animal calls and holiday trivia. All the chattering teeth at the swan swim.

All the ones of Luke. The man was photogenic as anything.

And obstinate, walled-off.

Wounded.

She tucked her blanket around herself and curled farther into one of the chairs by the fire in her cabin. What was her next step here? Today they had the

Eleven Pipers Piping Icing activity and tomorrow was the traditional Christmas Eve open house. She'd be done her duties.

Her throat ached at the thought. In volunteering, she'd expected to feel useful, to prove herself. She hadn't expected to fall further in love with the place. It was more than holiday magic. She'd discounted the relationship between the lodge and the land it sat on when she put together her original business plan.

Finding something good in something different.

She'd been so off base, adhering to rules instead of letting love take her somewhere new. Was she doing the same thing with the lodge, too? Could she keep the Emersons' conservationist spirit while focusing on the romantic roots her grandmother had planted?

She stared at some of the shots of decor she'd worked on, searching for an eco-friendly angle in the glamor she'd envisioned. Maybe she could offer different packages to attract and serve some of their existing populations. Adventure-themed, or nature-based, or zero-waste. Play up the luxurious, spa-and-gourmet-food bachelor and bachelorette party retreats, *and* offer fishing packages. She could even offer to keep Luke's precious tackle room intact by contracting an extension to be built to house a spa.

Excitement filled her, and she poured herself into the new ideas, slotting images into place, organizing themes and letting herself run wild with the possibilities.

She opened the next file, and her heart screeched

to a halt. Luke's and her "engagement" shots. Gray eyes, looking down on her with all the affection and caring of the fiancé he was pretending to be. Oh, God, did she include that one? Would he hate it?

Driven by impulse, she threw it onto a slide titled "Engagement Services." Yeah, it was intimate, but if he and Hank were going to see her whole vision, they had to see the emotion of it.

Hours later, her eyes ached and her body buzzed with satisfaction. She'd put together a crisp, professional PowerPoint, connected to what Hank and Luke loved about the place. This was it. How she'd win them over. It might not win her Luke's heart—not if he wasn't willing to face his pain, to let her support him while he healed—but it could win her his trust in terms of the lodge.

There were still so many images left, though. All the moments of festive joy. And poor Hank, having missed out on it all.

An idea sparked. As much as she loved her Power-Point, it was a business tool, not something to do with memories. Logging onto an online photo service in Bozeman, she sent off a raft of files to be printed. After cookie decorating, she could drive out and pick them up, and arrange them in a photo album for Hank.

She grinned to herself. After Luke announced the winner of the tree-decorating contest tomorrow, she could give Hank his gift and show them the presentation before heading to her parents' for Christmas Eve dinner.

Setting her computer aside, she stood, limbs ach-

ing from working so long. She needed to get ready
to decorate some cookies.

To face Luke, too. He'd only nodded at her when
they'd crossed paths at breakfast this morning. She
spent extra care getting ready, pulling on an A-line
dress printed with gingerbread people. A special purchase for today, and it matched her red heels to a T.
She curled her hair, too, and chose her favorite red
lipstick.

She'd promised to be here and be festive, damn it.
No matter how he'd walked off last night. She'd show
him her ideas tomorrow. They'd still end things, but
on a better note.

Her stomach lurched.

End things.

God, she wanted to figure out where all his raw
wounds still were. He needed to find happiness,
whether it included her or not. Even if he still decided they weren't right for each other, she hated the
idea of him living his life alone and hurting.

He's got to figure it out himself.

True. Maybe, though, there was a way to hold him
while he worked through it.

Nerves crowded her throat as she made her way
to the lodge and entered through the back door. The
scent of sugar cookies wafted through the air. A
shadow moved at the unlit end of the long, sparsely
decorated employee hallway. A familiar shape, one
she'd learned the angles and lines of during their
few, intense nights.

Luke's head jerked up from whatever notice he was reading on the bulletin board.

"Hey." His eyes swept from her hair to her shoes, gleaming in appreciation. He jammed his hands into the pockets of his jeans. "Where've you been?"

"Working on something." She wasn't ready to talk to him about it, not until she'd finished it.

His awkward smile made her want to pry, ask what was on his mind.

No. She'd had enough of him snapping at her about getting too personal yesterday.

"Before we get ourselves covered with icing…" He brushed a thumb along her cheek. She held back from nuzzling his palm, or better yet, leaning in for a kiss. "I'm sorry."

"For what?"

"Lashing out at you yesterday. Using it as an excuse not to spend the night with you. We only have a couple more days until Christmas, and I wasted one of them because I was licking my wounds."

"You're allowed to do that, Luke. Lick your wounds, that is. I wasn't so thrilled you deflected. Even though you had a point."

A breath shuddered from his beautiful mouth. "Maybe it's time I stop."

Edging closer, she snagged one of his hands with both of hers. Strong, warm fingers stroked the inside of her wrist. Tingles raced along her skin.

"Stop what, exactly?"

"Hiding behind my breakup with Cara."

She chewed on her lip. What did he mean? Moving forward alone? Being open to relationships?

The door to the dining hall flung open. The banquet captain, who was working some extra hours to help with cookie decorating, barreled into the hall. "Oh, good. You're both here. Two of my staff called in sick. Mind pitching in with dinner, too?"

"Of course not," Emma said.

Luke nodded, a hint of disappointment crossing his face.

The banquet captain hurried off.

"Talk later?" he asked Emma.

"Yeah."

Later turned out to be close to ten o'clock.

Emma flopped onto the couch in the nook, her icing-streaked dress flouncing up from the crinoline. The dining hall was empty. Only the two-story Christmas tree lit the place, reflecting a prism of color and light in the front windows. Letting out a groan, she toed out of her shoes. "Major admission—those are not meant to be worn for a dinner shift."

"Ouch."

Her brows drew together. Where was the *I told you so*?

Luke pulled a matchbook out of his jeans pocket. He lit the tall white candles of the German Christmas candle pyramid gracing the table in front of the side window. The decoration was one of the biggest ones Emma had ever seen, from the partridge and other birds on the top tier to the dancers and pipers and drummers on the bottom.

"Give it a minute," he said. "The propeller thing will start to spin, and all the animals and people will start moving. I used to stare at it for hours when I was a kid."

She could picture a smaller version of him studying the piece in fascination as one of his grandparents explained the figures. One of those family traditions that transcended generations. "It's gorgeous."

He eased onto the end of the couch and took one of her feet in his big hands. Thumbs pressed into the aching arch, tiny points of heaven.

She moaned and slapped the cushion with a palm. "Too good, Luke."

A lazy smile played on his lips. "Anytime."

"What, no smug crack about my footwear?"

He shrugged. "If you like how they look, who am I to criticize?"

Rising on her elbows, she pinned him with a look. "You've been slagging off my shoes all week."

"And I've decided to stop."

"Why?"

His gaze dipped to his lap. "I think we've both seen the charms in each other's differences since the festival started."

"Oh, yeah?"

"Yeah. You're charming as hell, Emma. This skirt alone…" He pulled her into his lap, fluffing the layers of tulle with a teasing hand. His smile faltered.

She smoothed his beard with her thumbs. "What are you thinking about?"

"Last night you told me you wanted to meet me halfway. I...I don't know how to do that yet."

A lump filled her throat. "Oh, love..."

He paled.

She didn't regret the endearment. "I'm not going anywhere. I can be patient."

"I don't know if it will help."

"Of course it will. It'll give me time to get to know who you really are, too. I've clung to the labels I stuck on you in high school—cocky, intolerant—and didn't notice how you changed. Or how you were hurting."

"It's not about me *being* hurt. I—I'm always going to be the one who falls short. And I can't fail you, Emma. You're—" He cleared his throat. "Everything about you. You're light. The crackle in a cascading firework—the bright, exciting part. And I can't handle the thought of you losing that because of me."

Her head spun and she gripped his shoulders. "Why do you think it would be a guarantee?"

Mouth parted, he didn't say anything, just shook his head, almost imperceptibly.

"Shouldn't I be the one to get to decide if I'm willing to risk a broken heart?"

It was like he swept up the fragments of his shattered expression and formed them back into an opaque shield. "I promised myself I wouldn't hurt anyone else I loved."

"Loved?"

Flushing, he lifted a shoulder. "I'd get there. You would, too. We both know that."

And it sounded like…like perfection. No, not at all. Flawed, imperfect. But real. Worth it.

She stole a kiss, deep, laced with a hint of chocolate. "Maybe I'm not the only perfectionist in the room."

"What?"

"You're petrified of letting someone down. As much as I hate making mistakes and love to have all my ducks in a row—you've had me thinking. About what's reasonable, about compromising and accepting some flaws as workable instead of unforgivable."

Eyes squeezed shut, he dropped his head to the back of the couch.

She had to finish, even if he didn't want to hear it. "I know your hockey career didn't turn out how you wanted—does it make what you did manage to do any less valuable? And should a broken engagement to a person who didn't want a post-hockey life with you prevent you from enjoying that life yourself, with someone else? Maybe it's time to believe your best is good enough, and to make a new promise to yourself."

Come on, Luke. Say it. Say you promise to try.

"Emma…"

"Just consider it." Her stomach throbbed. Between her heart and her dreams, this man held too much of her future in his strong hands. She wanted to trust him. Not only with her feelings, the multiplying bloom of something far too close to love, but to follow through on his promise to listen to her. She took a calming breath. "I want to present my business plan to you and your grandfather tomorrow."

"On Christmas Eve?" He sounded puzzled.

"After you announce the winners of the tree competition. It— I've changed some things. If you can't meet me halfway with what we're feeling for each other, can you guarantee to keep an open mind when I show you the presentation?"

He stroked her face. "What have you changed?"

I've changed. Because of you. And I want to keep changing. "Some of my ideas."

A stormy gaze met hers. "I'll listen."

It should have made her smile. Even yesterday, it would have felt like a victory. Today, she wanted more. The lodge *and* Luke.

"Tonight's my last night staying here," she reminded him.

His sexy mouth pressed to her forehead. "One last hurrah?"

"Doesn't have to be. But if it is, it better be a good one."

"I know I can follow through in that arena."

"You're underestimating yourself," she whispered in his ear, nipping at the lobe. Spinning in his lap, she straddled him. Her skirts frothed around her. Only his jeans and her thin tights and panties separated them. He lifted his hips, and oh Lord, whoever designed denim to have seams and ridges right over a guy's package deserved a to be a billionaire. Need washed over her, wild and expansive, craving the heat of his stiff length.

"We should go back to the cabin before a guest wanders in," she said.

A finger traced her collarbone. "You have icing here."

"Lick it off."

Growling, he dipped his head. His tongue darted along her skin, lighting her on fire. "So sweet."

"There's more icing in the walk-in fridge." She gasped out a breath. "We could steal it. Take it back to my bed."

His gaze darkened. "And frost more cookies."

"If you're hungry." Her lips met his. A hint of sugar flavored his mouth. "I am."

"You don't like getting messy, Emma."

"I know." She swallowed, hating the tightness at the back of her tongue. "I will for you, though."

Luke woke up early on Christmas Eve, arms full of Emma and heart racked with indecision. Predawn blackness rimmed the cabin's curtains. His brain refused to settle back to sleep. She'd pulled his T-shirt on in the night. Her body heated the fabric, no doubt infusing it with her sugary scent. A sensory memento of the last few days. Last night, flipping up her tease of a dress, driving into her until she moaned—she was a gift he didn't deserve to get.

She somehow had him wondering if he could follow through. The corners of his mouth curved up. She was something.

Maybe his *someone*.

Was he capable of that?

Argh. Today was not the day to be consumed by uncertainty. For the sake of the final festival event and giving Emma's presentation the consideration he'd promised, he had to keep his head clear. Not possible if he stayed in bed with her. The minute those eyes opened and latched on to him, he'd be gone, muddled until the sun went down.

With a quick press of lips to her forehead, he untangled himself and got out of bed. It was too dark to see where his underwear had ended up, so he pulled on his jeans and threw his flannel shirt on, leaving it unbuttoned. Gripping his boots by the laces, he used his cell as a light and carefully wrote a note on the pad of paper she had on the table by the window. He'd start today with a run, untangle his thoughts on some of the cleared backroads.

He ignored the urge to climb back into bed with Emma and headed for his half of the cabin.

Pounding the pavement would get her off his mind, guaranteed.

It was sure as hell cold enough to distract him, despite the layers he put on.

Three miles didn't do it.

Neither did five.

By mile nine, pleasured moans were still echoing in his brain, but he was gasping like a pug who needed nose surgery. Time to give up. The sun was peeking up over the trees to the east. He slogged his sweating, grumpy ass up the few steps to his grandfather's porch and let himself in.

Brody lounged at the kitchen table, wearing only

pajama bottoms and a frown. "Didn't think to see if I wanted to join you?"

Luke toed out of his shoes and headed for the sink, grabbing himself a glass. His legs shook from over-exertion. He needed something with electrolytes, not water. "Got any Gatorade?"

"No."

"Maybe Grandpa has something." A quick check in the cupboards came up empty.

Brody riffled through his backpack and tossed Luke a small plastic tube. "That's what I use."

Electrolyte tablets. "Dick. I asked you if you had something."

"No, you asked if I had Gatorade."

He flipped his cousin the bird and busied himself making and downing the drink. He put the glass in the dishwasher, groaning.

"Jesus, how far did you run?" Brody asked.

"Not far enough."

Brody eyed Luke's legs. "Any farther and you would have pulled a hammy."

"My hamstrings are golden." Lies. They burned like he'd finished a bag skate.

"And your head? Where's it at?"

The skin on the back of Luke's neck crawled. Too many coaches and therapists had asked him that question whenever he missed a pass, hit the crossbar, lost a championship game. And though Brody wasn't referring to the mental preparation necessary to excel at hockey, Luke still didn't have a good answer.

"Just thinking about today. Our last open house,

and then Emma wants to go over some things before she heads to the ranch."

His cousin paused, coffee cup halfway to his mouth. "Things?"

"A modified business plan, I think."

"On Christmas Eve?"

"She deserves our time," Luke said. "Worked her ass off these past couple weeks."

"Wrapped you around her finger while she was doing it, too."

Luke stiffened. "What would you know about it?"

"You've figured out how Halloran girls work, right? Diving into things at the expense of all else?"

"That's old news." And he did not need Brody throwing variables at him, clouding the situation even more. "Emma's driven, but she doesn't bounce from one thing to another like you've watched Bea do her whole life."

"This isn't about Bea."

He had a feeling his cousin's mood was more about Bea and her engagement than Brody would ever be willing to admit. "Isn't it?"

"No, it's about you," Brody said. "Are you sure Emma's interested in you for you, not for the lodge?"

"Emma wouldn't hook up with me for the sake of currying favor." Hell, it would be easier if he believed she *had* gotten involved with him to get an in. "She's honest. I trust her. She's been clear about why she wants to buy the lodge. And she's wanted it for a long time."

Her words last night, about promises and changing—she seemed to believe he could actually make her happy for more than a few days.

That would mean putting his own fears aside...

Brody crossed his arms. "One of two things will happen—either Grandpa decides not to sell to her, and she'll want nothing to do with you, or he does sell to her, and she'll become so absorbed with fixing the place up she won't have time for you."

"Damn, is the milk in your coffee sour this morning?"

Brody scowled. "Don't set yourself up to be left behind."

Luke choked out a laugh. "Rich advice, coming from you."

"What's that supposed to mean?"

The pictures on the wall behind Brody mocked Luke. His cousin accepting medals as both an athlete and a coach, interspersed with those of Hank holding the league trophy aloft and watching his number climb to the rafters. And Luke, newly drafted and holding the jersey he'd wear fewer than ten times. "You've made a career of leaving me in the dust."

The spoon clattered on the table. Brody slapped his palm over it, stopping the metallic rattle. "Excuse me?"

A door squeaked from down the hall, and Hank emerged. "If your grandmother were alive, she'd have your heads for yelling on Christmas Eve. What's all the racket about?"

"Luke's wound up about Emma and somehow blaming me for it," Brody grumbled.

Blood rushed from Luke's head and he forced himself to take a deep breath. It wasn't Brody's fault he'd achieved athletic success far beyond Luke's. "Never mind. I'm feeling like garbage after my run. I'm going to shower."

"What about the open house, son?" Hank asked. "And the tree competition winner?"

"Yeah, that's up next. Emma and I have it under control."

The open house, anyway.

At this rate, he'd never regain control over what was going on between them.

Chapter Fourteen

"You are one sexy candy cane, ma'am."

Luke's gruff murmur rippled from Emma's ear all the way to her core. She fanned her overheated face. She'd have loved to blame it on the body heat coming off all the people in ugly sweaters spinning around the room, but that was only enough to give her cheeks a glow.

The full rush of warmth was from Luke alone.

"This is my victory dress," she said.

"You're that sure your Brownies are going to be crowned the winners?"

"Yes. *And* I'm going to blow you away with my new ideas." She'd taken the last few pictures she needed of the crowd milling about, using them as stand-ins for wedding crowds. A few people were dancing by the Christmas tree—a bonus. She'd also dashed into the lodge office to print off a few last pictures to add to Hank's album. The pictures from the winning tree ceremony would have to be added later. She'd saved a few slots for any last memories.

"You blow me away, all right," Luke said. Hands slid around her waist, settling over the buttons on the cardigan she was wearing over another A-line dress, this one striped red, white and green.

"Careful. Rest those hands any lower and people are going to think we're hiding a Christmas surprise."

He chuckled.

"Oh, you laugh now, until we're the topic of conversation the next time you go into Peak Beans to grab a coffee."

"We might already be this week's gossip, Emma."

And until he was into more than a holiday fling, she shouldn't like it so much. Not the idea of being the newest story to light up Sutter Creek's gossip chain. *Definitely* not the idea of having a baby with him.

All of it made her heart melt and her legs feel wobbly. She would be proud to walk along the wooden sidewalks of the Main Street square, holding hands. And God, throw in a stroller? Yes, please. Luke would be an amazing father. Teaching a little girl to fish, boosting a miniature version of himself up high to put Hank's antique angel on top of the tree—way too easy to picture.

The gentle sway of his big body was mesmerizing, an easy side-to-side, in rhythm with the She & Him version of "The Christmas Waltz" playing over the dining hall's speakers. He sang quietly, completely in tune.

"I didn't know you could stay on key," she said. "Why is there no caroling day for the festival? We'll have to do that—" *Oof.* The reality of her plan walloped her in the gut. It didn't involve Luke or Hank. She'd never ask the older man to leave his cottage until he was ready, but going forward, it was going to be her project. It would muddy the waters to try to keep the Emerson brand involved at all.

"Singing in public is a big no," he said, giving her an out from finishing her thought.

"You just were."

"Only for you. It's my favorite Christmas song. I like the words."

About Christmas being a time when people fell in love?

I'd get there. You would, too.

She closed her eyes, not wanting to connect those dots. He hadn't said he was falling in love with her. He'd said he didn't want to. Today would be the last day they'd snuggle on the sidelines of a party. No more comfort from his arms, or the intimacy of having all his attention.

Time to stop letting the glow of tree lights and the lilt of the music lull her into believing in something he wouldn't let happen.

"Dance with me?" he asked.

Distance, Emma. She glanced over her shoulder out of the corner of her eye. "I'm not sure a man who sneaks out of my bed at the ass crack of dawn gets to mark up my dance card."

"I told you, I needed to clear my head."

"You say that as if *you're* the one who's about to lay all their life's dreams on the line."

He turned her to face him and cupped both her cheeks. "I know you're the one presenting, but I'm going to be there, too, needing to listen and try to be objective. And Emma—you must have figured out I have a hell of a bias when it comes to you."

"Is it wrong of me to be glad about that? To hope it'll shift things to go my way?"

Smiling, he kissed her.

"You know," Bea said, coming up from behind them. "Mom would be more annoyed you've been scarce this week, were it not for the promise of grandchildren."

"Go talk to Jason about it, then. This isn't going to lead to more Hallorans." Emma waved between Luke and her.

His hand flexed on her hip.

Why, she didn't think she wanted to know.

Bea's face darkened. "I can't talk to Jason—he's working. And I want to get home to Dad's eggnog, but I'm Gray's ride."

Their brother was on the other side of the party with a few of his firefighting compatriots, waiting for the reveal of the tree winner.

Emma bounced on her toes and checked the clock on the mantel. "About time for the announcement, right, Luke?"

He laughed. "Okay. You go ask everyone to meet outside by the trees. I'll get organized with the ribbons and the checks and will meet you out there in five minutes."

Emma made the announcement and gathered up her excited Brownies. They danced around the tree, hyped up on sugar and the magic of the holiday. A crowd of spectators waited out on the path.

A big hand landed on Emma's shoulder and squeezed.

"Hey, darlin'," Hank said. "These kids of yours look ready to climb the rafters."

One of the twins looked up at the exposed wooden beams. "Are we allowed, Mr. Emerson?"

He laughed. "Not a good idea." He refocused on Emma. "I've been thinking—"

"Merry Christmas, everyone." Luke, lights flashing on his Christmas tree sweater, spoke into the portable microphone and speaker he'd brought outside with him. "I'm told it's time to get to announcing so all these kids can get home and get ready for a special visitor tonight. As you know, we divide all the donations between the twelve charities and organizations. And for our final festival, Sutter Creek opened their wallets in an impressive way. Even the twelfth-place team will be going home with a healthy amount." He named a total far higher than the previous year. "Thank you for your generosity."

The Brownies squealed in unison.

Cammie tugged on Emma's arm. "We get our canoes, Ms. Emma!"

"We do." Emma leaned down and hugged each girl. "Might be able to update our tents, too, if we place high enough."

The crowd applauded. Oh, crud, she'd missed the announcement for the third-place team. Standing on her toes, she spotted the Canoe and Kayak Club celebrating around their tree.

"Are we going to win?" one of the Brownies whispered.

"Let's listen," Emma said.

Luke held up a big silver ribbon. "Our silver ribbon goes to the most colorful tree I think we've ever seen in twenty years—Emma Halloran and her Brownies."

"Second!" Most of the Brownies cheered and jumped around, except Cammie.

She tugged on the ends of her braids and frowned. "Second?"

"A result we can be proud of. We worked really hard," Emma said, nudging the twins to accept the ribbon from Luke. His smile was for her only, wide with pride and amusement. She'd have labeled it loving if she didn't know better. When Cammie hesitated, she added, "And it's important to be good sports."

When it came to trees, anyway. She wouldn't be so jovial if her presentation for Hank came in second place.

Luke announced the firefighters as the winners. She groaned. She'd never hear the end of that from Gray.

The applause eventually petered out. Luke's smile

turned sentimental. "On behalf of my grandfather and my cousin and all the staff, we want to say a huge thanks to all of you for attending all these years. It wasn't always easy to keep going after Grandma passed, but it was sure worth it. And this year, a special thanks to Emma for making our efforts flawless. It really meant…well, everything."

His throat bobbed and he caught her gaze, his expression full of yearning and uncertainty.

She could barely hear the clapping for the roaring in her ears. Her limbs were frozen in place.

Everything.

She wanted to be this man's everything.

Would he let himself want the same?

A half hour after Emma said goodbye to her Brownies, she stood in Hank's living room, trying to decide where to start. Her stomach was jumping around more than her troop had with their silver ribbon.

Hank relaxed in his armchair with Splotches stretched lazily on his lap. The feline fixed Emma with a golden stare, clearly not willing to move.

"Ten days and I've lost your loyalty?" Emma said. "Well…"

"She'll be yours again once you're back in your apartment," Hank said. "Though if you want me to keep her over Christmas while you're at your parents', I'm happy to."

"Thank you," Emma said. If all went well, Splotches would have to get used to living out here.

Emma planned to renovate one of the one-bedroom suites in the lodge for her own use rather than live off-property.

"You're clutching that book pretty tight, my girl," Hank said.

"Oh, right!" She passed him the red leather photo album.

He untied the sparkly ribbon. "Is this the presentation you've been talking about?"

"No." She took a seat on the couch. "That's on my phone. I'll project it on your television. This is a gift. For memory's sake." She squeezed his hand. "No matter what you decide about my offer, it was a real shame you missed most of the festival. I wanted to preserve it for you."

He opened the cover. His expression softened with every page he flipped, until his eyes glinted with moisture. "Emma, this is a delight."

"I'm glad you like it."

The front door opened. Luke came in, brushing icy flakes off his hair and beard and removing his gloves and boots.

"Holy Yukon Cornelius," she teased.

"Good thing we wrapped up," he said. "Snow's picking up. You'll need to be careful on the road, Em."

"Of course." So fricking bossy. But it was easy to see the caring intent behind it now.

Hank passed the album over to Luke, who sat on the opposite end of the couch from Emma.

"What's this?"

"A little something for your grandfather," she said. "Doesn't make up for him missing so many activities, but it at least preserves it."

"Wow." He stroked a finger over a shot of them stuck in the snow cave entrance. Nora had only been too happy to send it over. "Seems like a year ago."

"We did good work."

"Your grandma would have been impressed." Hank sighed. "If she was still alive, she'd be furious at me for considering a sale."

Gooseflesh rose on Emma's arms. She needed him to be receptive, not doubting retirement.

"She did see it staying in the family," Luke said quietly. "Always loved it bearing our name."

She whirled to face him. "She would have completely understood Hank's need to retire!" *Deep breath. Calm.* "Let me show you what I've come up with. I think Jenny would have gotten a kick out of it. Are we waiting for Brody?"

"He's at his mom's." Hank's tone tipped into sadness. "Doesn't feel the need to be a part of the decision."

A look crossed Luke's face, one Emma was getting better at reading. He so clearly believed he had to live up to some unrealistic image for the sake of his grandfather.

Hands shaking, she connected her phone and pulled up her slide deck. The title slide showed off two older photos—one of her grandparents on their wedding day, and one of Hank, Jenny, Luke and

Brody out on the river. The boys were small, holding a giant fish in four little hands.

"This river and these buildings are entwined with both our families. I rolled in here a little under two weeks ago, envisioning five-star glamor and getting my family name back on the title." She swallowed. This would only work if she didn't hold anything back. "I've struggled to feel seen in my family, and the Dawson family history on my mom's side is too often lost under the Halloran ranch domination. I want to fix that. But the more I worked with—" she sent Luke a smile, failing to keep it from wobbling "—*argued* with Luke, the more I knew it wasn't right to lose everything you've done, too."

She took her time with the following slides. Sketches of her dreams for the lodge renovations. All the new eco-friendly packages she'd come up with, subbing in the festival decor and crowds to show what a Christmas wedding could look like. She focused on Hank because Luke's scrutiny was a burning spotlight, singeing her whenever she made direct contact with it.

The last slide was one of the pictures of her and Luke during their "engagement" shoot. She still couldn't get over his tender expression.

"The lodge can be romantic *and* have environmental significance," she finished.

Hank's eyes widened. "That's some picture."

"Even we got swept up by the magic of the season," she said.

Luke blinked at the TV. Vulnerability flickered

across the rugged angles of his face. "Didn't we, now."

"The magic of the season," Hank echoed, absent-mindedly petting Splotches. "You'd keep the festival going?"

She shook her head. "Not as a whole—holiday weddings are too big a draw to block off two weekends. I'd spread the most popular events throughout December."

Hank's mouth twisted. He flicked through a few of the pages of the photo album. His hand stilled over a shot she'd snagged of Luke skating fast enough around the frozen lake to blow his hair back.

The cuckoo clock on the wall ticked, half the speed of Emma's racing pulse.

She couldn't take the silence. "Thoughts?"

"Darlin'…"

Just like she'd been able to read Luke's expression, she could read his grandfather's, and the regret there—*no*. "Please, Hank."

"It's too much." His voice cracked. "All these lodge renovations, the programming switch, the Emerson name… And I can't let this year be the last Twelve Days."

The words crashed into Emma like a rockslide. So definitive. So *wrong*. She grasped at one last option. "What about a slow transition—"

"I don't want to lead you on any longer," Hank said. "Jenny wouldn't have wanted that, either."

She blinked at him, hoping to catch some last dreg of hope to grip onto, but all she saw was his resolute need to protect his memories of the person he loved. *Same thing I've been trying to do.* Why couldn't he see how her new plan did both?

"Grandpa," Luke said, voice measured. "When I mentioned Grandma's wishes, I didn't mean we're obligated to abide by them. Emma's got some wonderful ideas, and—"

"Wonderful or not, I'm not ready," Hank said. "You offered to take over, Luke—do you still want to? Would you do that for me, son?"

His eyes widened, confused and cautious. "I honestly thought—" He cleared his throat. "I didn't think you trusted me to do it."

"I trust you, Luke. I don't want you to resent the place, though."

"I wouldn't." Half his mouth curved up. "Wow."

She wanted to curl into a ball on the floor. He was *happy* about this?

"You'll do it?" Hank said.

Luke dodged her gaze and blew out a breath. "If— if it means protecting what you've built, Grandpa… I mean, I did want…"

It was like her insides imploded. Everything she'd worked for over the past years, months, weeks, sucked into a black hole of Luke Emerson finally getting the approval he wanted at the expense of her failure.

Fighting to keep her lunch down, she gathered her things. "I guess there's nothing else to say."

"Emma." Luke stood. "Wait."

"I need to get over to my parents'. My family is

probably wondering why I'm taking so long." *Maybe.* Her family had noticed her festival-related absences, but they were getting along without her. She held in a sob. "Merry Christmas."

She threw on her coat and ran out the door. It would be so much worse to let him see her cry.

"Emma, wait!" Luke jogged in pursuit, catching her arm right as her feet hit the cleared path.

She whirled on him. Wind gusted, blowing up her skirt and through her tights. She shivered. "Why bother? You got what you wanted. You planted the seed that your grandmother wouldn't want Hank to sell. You've been waiting for him to agree you should take over. And as much as I know his request is amazing for you, I'm not in the mood to sit around and watch you celebrate."

"Yeah, about that. I don't know—"

"You're getting what you wanted, protecting your family legacy." Her nose stung like she'd inhaled a cloud of chlorine. "You didn't hear a thing I said in my proposal or see what I was trying to do. Didn't see *me*."

His mouth went haggard. "I did, honey. I *do*. I see how you're incredible, and—"

"Not enough for you to believe in me." Fat flakes swirled around them, a snow globe world mirroring the chaos churning in her core.

He jammed a hand into his thick hair. "Emma, I'm not sure you heard me, either. I didn't say yes yet."

"You will."

He cupped her elbow. "I need more than a minute

to think about it. To talk to my grandpa about my options *and* your proposal."

"We've talked enough." She backed up a step, hugging her purse to her chest. "You told me you'd end up hurting me, and I didn't listen. Good thing I didn't let myself fall in love with you, because I'd have lost my heart, too."

A big damn lie. She spun and hurried for her car. She had to get away before she confessed the truth.

Luke forked a bite of Brody's Christmas Eve lasagna into his mouth. He swallowed, gagging a little.

"Sorry my dinner offends your delicate sensibilities," his cousin said.

"The food's fine." Emma's accusations were the problem, constricting, pushing him to the edge of being ill.

You told me you'd end up hurting me, and I didn't listen.

Brody shook his head in clear disbelief. "You're really going to quit your job and run this place?"

"One of us needs to." Luke twirled a thick noodle with a fork, misjudging the length. It spun off the tines and landed on the plate with a splat.

"Why?" Brody asked.

"Who else is going to do it?" Luke said.

"Uh, Emma?"

Guilt gripped him. She'd sacrificed these past couple weeks. Put forward a logical, carefully crafted solution, too, but because of Luke mentioning his grandmother and the Emerson name, his grandfather had only given lip service to the presentation.

Goddamn it. He'd needed time to think, and she'd made all sorts of assumptions. If she'd only been willing to discuss it. Instead, she'd assumed the worst and had cut ties, like she always did in a relationship.

Of course she made assumptions. You might not have outright agreed when you were offered the opportunity, but you didn't turn it down.

And now, with Emma gone—was there anything to do but accept what now felt like a consolation prize?

"You don't sound excited about taking over, son," Hank interjected. "I thought—"

"I asked you for the opportunity, Grandpa. I'm not going to back out." Learning his grandfather trusted him had filled him with a level of pride he hadn't felt in a long time. Maybe never.

But at the cost of giving up your career and betraying Emma?

It wasn't giving up his career. Not exactly. Protecting the lodge was about his passion for the environment. Wasn't it?

If it was, this decision would feel right. He'd willingly made the offer months ago.

Accepting it now felt like rubbing against coarse sandpaper. He gritted his teeth.

"You asked, yeah, but a fair amount's changed since then," Hank said.

"Such as…"

"That picture, the one at the end of Emma's presentation."

"What picture?" Brody asked around a mouthful of pasta.

The one where I looked at Emma like she held my world in her hand. He ignored his cousin and cocked an eyebrow at his grandfather. "What about it?"

"I've never seen you look at a woman the way I looked at your grandmother."

"Emma and I are not like you and Grandma." Luke stabbed his lasagna.

Brody sat back in his chair. "You could be."

"There's no way to have her and this." Luke waved toward the front window. The lodge was barely visible through the thick snowfall. "Not without some serious overhauls. She really tried to meet us halfway. Merging her vision and ours—it was gorgeous. You can't deny it, Grandpa. There was no way to watch her weave her vision and not be impressed. And I—"

"You what?" Brody said.

"I was ready to tell her I thought we should go for it, and then Grandpa offered me the job. And I froze."

"It's not a hockey game." Brody laid his fork on his plate. "You don't need split-second reactions."

"I shouldn't have gotten distracted by Grandpa's offer." He looked at his grandfather, who wore a wary expression. "When you dug in your heels, I should have pressed harder. Shouldn't have sat there, letting you shut her down."

Hank's concern turned to confusion. "I thought you wanted to protect the property. You've taken up conservation as a career, for Pete's sake. You've been the one telling me weddings are ridiculous, and the ways the river will suffer if the lodge isn't here."

"I know." He rubbed his temples. He wanted to rewind time back to earlier in the day when he and Emma were swaying on the side of the open house. When he'd sung a little and earned the sweetest smile. If he could just press Pause...

Pause won't work. He wanted to move *forward* with her.

Chapter Fifteen

Luke propped his elbows on the table and tented his fingers, trying to make sense of how to explain his change of heart to his grandfather. His thoughts were scraps of sentences, jumping around too fast to grab. The river, their family, Emma's family... And more than any of it, not wanting to wake up in the morning without her.

The pictures on the wall behind Hank, of medals and jerseys and Stanley Cups over his shoulder—they were still making fun of Luke's efforts.

That's the past.

Man, the past hurt sometimes.

"Protecting the lodge was supposed to be about preserving our family name," he said. "Everything *you've* built."

Hank crossed his arms. "And?"

"And none of it made me good enough! None of it *will* make me good enough. No matter how hard I try. I thought the lodge would be enough—"

Brody followed Luke's gaze to the pictures on the wall. "It's not your Stanley Cup, after all?"

"Being offered the lodge in no way feels like a win."

"Hang on." Hank held up a hand. "What do you mean, making you good enough?"

Luke pointed at the wall. "Between the two of you, this family has enough trophies to swamp a canoe. And I was always grasping. And Cara kicked me while I was down, not wanting to be with me if I didn't have an NHL contract—"

"Son."

He couldn't handle the pitying tone.

"No. I didn't bring it up to garner sympathy. But I've been trying to live up to our family name for my whole life. After I failed out of hockey, I thought wilderness management was the way to do that. My job and the lodge. Now, I want to find another way. To give Emma a chance to make her dream come to life."

"Hold up. This has nothing to do with wilderness management and renovations and business plans." Hank jolted to his feet, sending his chair back with a clatter. "This is about my damn flesh and blood not feeling good enough to call himself an Emerson. You busted your ass to make it to the pros. Got drafted. Worked as hard as you could. And you did the same when you came home. That is all I could ever expect of you. You wanna know what I talk about when I go into town? It isn't my trophies. It's the animals you protect, and the cases you solve. And yeah, I talk about Brody and his medals, but no more than you, Luke. I could not be prouder of you. Even when you're being a jackass."

"A jackass?"

"The definition of one. You were going to let all that get in the way of finding love with a hell of a woman."

A breath shuddered from Luke's lungs. "Still couldn't be prouder of me?"

"Of course."

Had he really been reading things wrong for so long? Misunderstanding his worth, his value to the family? "And if I tell you I don't want to run the lodge and we'd be stupid not to sell to Emma?"

Hank gripped the counter with one hand and coughed into his elbow.

"Need your inhaler, Grandpa?" Brody asked.

"Yes." Hank held out a hand and took the medication when Brody passed it to him. "Son of a bitch. These lungs."

"Pneumonia is not a small thing," Luke said.

"You need to retire sooner rather than later," Brody added, catching Luke's gaze.

Luke lifted an eyebrow.

Brody didn't say anything, but the look in his eyes—a guilty apology—said enough.

"We can't let this place go, though. Not entirely. I can't do it," Hank said.

"And I can't accept your inertia." Emma was worth trying for. Every time. She'd talked about the forgivable mistakes in a relationship, and the things that were forever roadblocks. This had to be the former. He could prove being with her and being willing to make mistakes would always be better than not being with her at all.

Pieces of her plan bounced around in his head. It was all about coming together to celebrate unity. *Partners.*

Clarity burst through his tangled thoughts. "What about joining together? Emma managing the place, planning those perfect wedding days she keeps going on about. On behalf of both our families."

Slippers shuffling on the linoleum, Hank made his way out of the kitchen and into the living room, where he sat in his chair. Splotches jumped onto his lap. Luke shook his head. Emma wasn't ever getting her cat back at this rate.

Hank stared at the Christmas tree. "Joint ownership?"

"Yes."

Brody let out a thoughtful noise.

"Yeah, yeah, Brody. Halloran girls pour themselves into things at the expense of all else, I know." Luke left his dinner on the table and stood next to the tree to make sure his grandfather couldn't avoid looking his way. "Wouldn't that be a solid quality in a business partner?"

"It would," Brody admitted.

"Grandpa?" Luke said.

Amusement lit the older man's eyes. "You really love her."

"I think I do." His neck got hot, and he glanced to the side, studying the tree. Emma had decorated this tree. All the glittery ornaments held places of honor—front and center. And his grandmother's German glass treasures, too. Every year, his grandfather packed those up like they were more precious than a priceless painting sitting in a museum somewhere.

No matter how many times Luke screwed up, he'd still want to find his own precious things with Emma. The things they'd pack up in tissue paper when they were seniors with grandchildren and more memories than they knew what to do with.

"All right, boys. If you both think this is the way to go." Hank's mouth twisted and he petted the cat with a shaking hand.

"You don't look convinced," Luke said.

"I'll get there."

"This is the right decision." Excitement sparked in Luke's veins. "You'll let me ask Emma?"

"As long as it's fifty-fifty, and follows what she said today, then yes."

Luke started pacing. "I need to plan something as well thought-out as the presentation she made for us." He knew the exact place to try to win her over. He needed chairs, and some of the evergreen boughs and vintage tinsel she'd been strewing everywhere.

With any luck, or maybe some of the holiday charm she loved so much, he'd be able to convince her to love him enough to stick with him, flaws and all.

"Brody, I need your help. Put on your coat."

"But my long winter's nap," his cousin complained, linking his fingers over his flat belly.

"Consider it my Christmas present."

A mechanical buzz cut into Emma's sleep. She burrowed under the covers, trying to block out the annoying whine. Freaking ranch work, even on Christmas morning.

The racket sounded extra loud today, given how little sleep she'd managed to cobble together. She hadn't told her family about the outcome of her pitch last night. Everyone had been soused in nostalgia and her dad's eggnog, and she hadn't wanted to bring down the mood. Between sharing too much red wine with Bea and mentally replaying her failed pitch and argument with Luke, she'd tossed and turned long after her mom and dad announced the "kids" needed to hit the sack so they could finish playing Santa.

She loved how her parents insisted on still having stockings for everyone. It was a tradition she couldn't wait to start with her own family.

If I ever have one.

At this rate, she'd be stuck making a stocking for Splotches for the next fifteen years, provided the cat was willing to leave Hank's cottage.

The droning hum got louder, until it sounded like it was right outside her window.

It stopped.

Thank God.

She wasn't on chore duty until later in the morning—she'd pulled Christmas dinner detail—so she had at least two more hours until she'd need to pretend to be happy while opening presents. She closed her eyes, desperate for more sleep.

For an escape from her thoughts, too.

Click.

Something hit her window.

Oh, for crying out—

Click, click.

She clenched her jaw, jammed on her glasses and went to the window.

A shower of what sounded like tiny pebbles hit the glass. She flung the curtains back. If Gray or Nora had decided to wake her up since they were up with the cows, she'd—

Not Gray or Nora.

Luke, standing next to a snowmobile, staring up at her second-floor window. He'd triggered the motion light on the side of the house. The beam spotlighted his big frame, his messy hair and the helmet in one of his gloved hands. He wore an open overcoat, over a…suit? With snowmobile boots?

And his face… Delicious as always. Enraging, too. His resolute expression matched the one Hank had worn last night when he turfed Emma's proposal. She'd had about enough of stubborn Emerson men.

Even when they showed up all bearded, burly and in a tie.

He motioned for her to open her window.

The metal frame squeaked as she slid it sideways. She got right up close to the screen and looked down at him. "What are you doing here?"

Only a whisper; Bea and Jason were in the room under hers, and they didn't have to get up early, either.

"I have something to show you," he said in an equally low voice.

"Now?"

"Yes." A plea. His eyes pled, too. Dark and desperate.

It snagged at her aching core. Nothing was going to happen between them, but she couldn't snap her fingers and be done with her feelings for him. She wasn't built that way. It was going to take time to get over him, to recalibrate after losing her chance at the lodge. And for her to start healing, he needed to get the hell off her parents' lawn.

"I have breakfast," she hissed.

He checked his phone. "No, you don't. Brody asked Bea, and she said you wouldn't be eating until eight."

She forced herself to relax her jaw—no need to crack a molar on a day when no dentists were working. "Exactly. You don't get to roll in here at six a.m. on freaking Christmas morning. You barely bothered to hear what I had to say yesterday."

The window under Emma's slid open.

"We're trying to sleep. Declare your love for each other somewhere else," Bea snapped.

"Sorry," Emma said. "And I'm not declaring—"

"*I* am," Luke said.

Emma's heart rate doubled. "What?"

"It's why I'm here. To tell you I love you."

Her knees wobbled, and she gripped the windowsill. "Since when?"

"I don't know when," Luke said. "But it's real. And I'm sorry. I figured some things out, and—"

"Finish figuring them out somewhere else!" Bea shouted. "For the love of gingerbread, Emma, if you two don't shut up I'm taking your Lululemon hoodie back to Seattle with me."

Emma blinked. Lululemon hoodie? Huh. She'd actually asked for one of those.

Luke's mouth lifted at one corner. "Put on something warm and join me on the porch."

"How long is this going to take?" she said.

"A lifetime, hopefully—"

Her head spun. "A *lifetime*?"

"Come talk to me down here, Emma. Before your sister raids your parents' gun safe and peppers my ass with bird shot."

Could she do this again, give him another chance to explain himself and end up feeling like she did last night? Her chest still throbbed with the realization she'd never be able to see her vision come to life at the lodge, but it was nothing compared to how awful it had felt when Luke had silently stood by. *Love*, though. And *lifetime*. Her inner romantic wanted to latch on to his words and never let go.

"Five minutes," she said. "Only because it's Christmas."

She quickly brushed her teeth, threw on enough layers to survive a trip to the North Pole and crept down the stairs. Her reflection glared at her from the hallway mirror. And her bedhead would *not* do. She pulled on a thin beanie and her parka and boots and let herself onto the porch. The cold nipped at her cheeks, helped clear her head.

Face-to-face, she could remind Luke of all the reasons they couldn't make this work, and retreat to her cocoon until breakfast. She groaned. Breakfast was going to be miserable now. By the time the platters of bacon and waffles landed on the table, everyone would know about her early-morning visitor. She'd have to explain Luke's presence, which would require admitting her pitch had fallen short and she'd been unable to articulate her vision to the people she loved.

Tears stung her eyes. She blinked them away, watching Luke crunch through the snow. He paused at the bottom of the four-stair rise. And he looked at her with so much hope.

Her tears turned hot, angry. How dare he look at her with such audacious optimism? Hope was *her* thing, and he and Hank had ripped it away—

"Merry Christmas, honey."

She took a breath and ignored the sexy gravel in

his voice. "You needed to drag me out of bed for *holiday wishes*?"

"Yeah." He stroked a hand over his beard. "And to show you something. *Before* breakfast and presents."

"Because…"

A nervous smile played on his lips. "You left disappointed last night—I can't not try to fix it. I love you, Emma. I'm not sure if I'll ever walk through a day not worried about letting you down, but I'll take the chance, if it means having you in my life."

She wrapped her arms around her middle, desperate to stop the ache in her core from taking over every cell in her body. "How can you love me if you don't see what really matters to me? Yesterday, what mattered was for you to support me. Not to take a job you don't really want."

"I know. I screwed up. And you walked away before I could make it right."

Walked away. Like so many people had in his life. And yet, he was still here…

"Would you give me the chance to show you a new idea I came up with?" His eyes gleamed silver in the porch light.

Who knew what he was getting on about with new ideas, but he was right about one thing. "I did leave in the middle of a conversation. I was hurt. Devastated, really. Still numb this morning."

"I know. And I want to make it up to you. Come with me for an hour or so. I really did see the beauty in what you pitched, and—well, I have some ideas, too."

The morning silence was so quiet, it was like shouting in her ears... Wait. Not silent anymore. Voices chattered from the direction of the barn. Nora harassing Gray, and their mother defending the baby of the family.

Her stomach throbbed. "They're headed this way."

"Let's escape. Trivia night, you claimed to love snowmobiling."

He'd put her preference to memory? Her chest warmed a little.

"Emma!" Gray jogged over. "You're way late for chores."

"Yeah, not why I'm up," she said.

Whistling low, Gray gave Luke a once-over, stomped off his boots and climbed to the porch. "What's with the getup, man?"

"I needed to ask your sister something."

"You're getting *engaged*?" The question came from Nora, still ten feet away.

"No," Luke said. "Though it's a nice idea."

"Luke." The idea *would have* been nice prior to him shattering her last fragment of hope yesterday. "Stop."

"Nope," he said, smile nervous.

Emma's mom brought up the rear of the entirely unwelcome trio. "Emma? Luke? Is everything okay?"

Emma opened her mouth to say she was fine.

But I'm not.

Maybe if she wanted her family to see her, she needed to be honest with them instead of hiding behind her everything's-under-control facade.

"No," she said, not bothering to keep her voice from wobbling. "Everything isn't okay. Hank's decided not to sell. I lost my chance."

Her mom inhaled sharply. "Maybe it's for the best, sweetie."

"It absolutely isn't," she said. "You know the only thing I want for Christmas? For everyone to see how important this was to me. It *really* mattered. It was my chance to put all the dreams Grammy and I talked about in motion. To have my own thing, like Nora has the ranch and Jack is a freaking hero and Bea beats to her own drum and Gray can do no wrong—"

"Hey!" Gray protested.

"And it's all moot now," Emma finished.

"Except it *isn't*." Luke climbed the stairs and stood in front of her, cupping her cheeks with his gloved hands. The fabric chilled her cheeks. "Honey, please."

"Please, what?" Nora's hands went to her hips. "Are you and your grandpa jerking Emma around? How could you see her business plan and not think it was a good idea?"

Emma raised her eyebrows at her sister. "As if *you've* ever taken the time to read my business plan."

"I read it last night," Nora said. "Borrowed your phone when my battery died, and your slide deck was open. It's an incredible plan, Emma. And if Luke and Hank aren't interested, it's their loss. If you really want to create an eco-friendly wedding resort, let's talk about how to make it happen at the ranch."

Light poked through the cracks in Emma's middle. It wasn't exactly her plan, but her sister was meeting her halfway in a manner she never had. Her head spun. "I'll... *Wow*, Nora."

"I *can* see how incredible Emma's ideas are." Luke threw his hands up. "How *she's* incredible. I want to prove it to her, but I can't do that on this porch."

Their audience peered at him with suspicion.

"She was ours first, Luke. And until she tells us otherwise, we get first dibs." Georgie faced Emma. "You're in a tough place, in the middle. And you've been so damn independent—it was easy to leave you to your own devices. Did we all make you feel like you were lost in the shuffle?"

Breath catching at her mom's words, Emma could only nod.

"You're the balance, Emma. The middle point we all hang off. So much a part of us we miss it sometimes. I'm sorry, sweetie." Georgie flung her arms around her, a strong, warm hug infused with mom love.

Emma's eyes started stinging again. Hugging her mom back, she sniffled. Her wobbling stomach settled a bit. She did have her family, even if they weren't perfect all the time. "I love you, Mom."

"I love you, too."

"Not the first person to tell you that this morning," Luke grumbled.

Pushing up her glasses, Emma took in her family's curious expressions and Luke's impatient longing. He *had* told her he loved her. And he'd admitted he was in the wrong and had shown a hell of a lot of passion for her... All Grammy's gold standards.

And make sure you're *open to surprises, Emma dear.*

Oof. Luke was right about her selective listening—she'd been ignoring the most important advice of all.

She took a step closer to him and slid her hand in his. "Luke does have dibs on me this morning. For an hour or so. I'll be back for breakfast."

Her mom stroked her back with a loving hand. "Take the time you need."

"I'm not promising to save you any bacon." Nora smirked, disappearing into the house.

"I'll take my chances," Emma said.

"You should take your chances with Luke, too. My gut says he's worth it." Gray studied them with seriousness she wasn't used to seeing from him. "And I will save you bacon."

He waved their mom into the house and then followed her in, closing the door.

"Save me bacon, my ass," Emma said ruefully. "He's a liar."

Luke still had her hand. He squeezed, strong and sturdy through their gloves. His gaze was eager and genuine and everything she'd wanted him to be last night. "So, let's hurry."

Chapter Sixteen

It took them fifteen minutes to cross the Halloran property. Fifteen long minutes of clinging to his back, her arms around his broad torso. Catching whiffs of woodsy warmth through the smells of snow and machine exhaust.

Once over the property line, he steered them onto a trail to the lake.

"It's too early to go skating," she yelled over the engine's roar.

"Tell that to the person who scheduled all my early hockey practices!"

She smiled against his overcoat. It was good to hear him talking about the sport he'd loved.

He slowed the machine and parked at a trailhead.

The moon was still up, and it shone across the new carpet of white on the lake.

"Close your eyes," he instructed. "I'll hold your arm. The trail is clear—you won't sink into the snow too badly."

She sent him a questioning look.

His mouth tilted. "Let me surprise you."

Her heart skipped. Holding out her arm, she shut her eyes.

Snow swished off branches in the forest. She expected it to get inside her boots, too, but it didn't. Whatever trail he was taking her on was plowed. It didn't crunch like snow under her feet, though. Weird. Wind swirled around them, biting her cheeks. Anticipation burned in her belly. And Luke's hand was steady on her elbow as he guided her along.

"Surprises are the best and the worst, and after yesterday, I don't know how much more I can handle."

"Almost there."

A few more steps, and he stopped her. He jogged what sounded like a few yards behind her.

"Okay, open," he said.

She did, blinking. They were in the clearing where her grandparents had gotten married. All the snow had been packed firm, and there were rows and rows of folding chairs, with cockeyed velvet bows hanging where pew decorations would usually go. A hideous olive green carpet runner bisected the chairs.

"Did you steal that from the front hall of the lodge?"

"Yeah."

She spun to face him, mind reeling. "You… You planned a wedding? Is this for *us*?"

"No!" He cleared his throat. "Well, not for today."

He'd taken off his overcoat. Whoever had done the tailoring on his suit had earned their pay, because the lines were cut perfectly for his broad shoulders and strong thighs. The arch behind him, the one he'd built, framed his tall body. Evergreen swags and glittery tinsel hugged the thick crossbeam and side posts.

Her breath caught. "You decorated the arbor."

"Nothing like you will be able to do, but I did my best."

"All your bad memories, though. You built the arch for—"

"I built it for something I had to go through to get where I am today." He shifted his weight from side to side. "I can turn it into something good."

Warmth spread through her.

But him comparing his effort to her own decorating skills—*like you will be able to do*—made no sense. "I'm confused."

"You said you wanted to plan perfect days for people."

Her throat constricted. "Which got rejected."

He closed the distance between them, and held out a small wrapped box.

Is it…? Fingers shaking, she tore at the gold paper. She lifted the lid. *Oh. Not a ring.* "A…key?"

"Unlocks the front door to the lodge."

She fumbled with the box. "For me?"

"Yes. For—hopefully—our new business partner."

A shiver racked her limbs. "Wh-what?"

Tender fingers stroked a lock of hair off her cheek. His chest rose and he blew out a long stream of air. "It feels wrong not to have the lodge connected to my family. But what would you say about sharing?"

Heart racing, Luke held his breath. The rest of his life was going to pivot on Emma's answer. It was bigger than getting let go from his hockey team or getting dumped by his fiancée or getting hired by Fish, Wildlife and Parks. Emma eclipsed it all.

Her eyes were wider than the moon hanging over the mountains. A hint of deep blue edged the tops of the trees to the east, promising a bright holiday morning once the sun finally showed itself.

He wanted to spend that morning with the woman in front of him. And tonight, and tomorrow, and the next day... He could be enough for her.

She clutched the box, teeth working her lower lip.

When she finally relaxed her mouth, it was red around the edge, as if he'd kissed her, hard. He *would* get the chance to savor her lips again.

Taking her free hand in both of his, he said, "It's a lot to think about."

"I'm not sure what exactly I *am* thinking about. What kind of business partnership? I wouldn't be much help running the lodge as is. Nor is it what lights me on fire."

"I know. I'm not suggesting the status quo. I want to see people using this clearing and the arbor I built.

My family wants to share ownership, but the vision of the place would be all yours."

Her mouth gaped.

"Actually, 'all yours' isn't wholly accurate. Your presentation yesterday, Emma… You kept a sense of romance and also honored what's important to me and my family. I'm sorry I didn't properly express how impressed I was, and that Grandpa turned you down."

Her hand tightened around his. "I'm sorry I walked away. Too many people have done that to you."

He shook his head. "It forced me to open up to my family, and realize I've held myself back. I'll inevitably disappoint you some days. Doesn't make *me* a disappointment, though. You helped me see it's different." He leaned in and kissed her, a light brush. "I'm not the man you saw yourself being with, but I could work on becoming him."

"You don't need to be anyone you're not. All my ideas of what I thought I wanted in 'the one'—they were foolish. Empty, compared to loving someone who's willing to give and grow and risk."

"I'll do those things for you."

"*With* me." She hugged his chest, burying her face in the crook of his neck like she'd been handcrafted to fit there. "I—I love you."

The words sparked in his belly like the fireworks they would set off at the lodge on New Year's Eve. Cupping the back of her head with one hand and settling his other palm on the small of her back, he held her, needing to make it clear he'd never let her go. "I love you, too."

"I didn't ever expect to hear you say that."

"I plan to say it so much, you'll get tired of hearing it."

"Never," she said. "I also can't believe you convinced your grandfather to work with me."

"I didn't. You did, by knocking our socks off yesterday. I only helped him see a way to work around his fear of change."

Leaning back, she caught his gaze. It was too dark for the green of her eyes to stand out. Like waking up in the middle of the night and seeing those eyes blink open. It'd be hard not to make love to her in those moments. He grinned. They'd have to get a top-of-the-line coffeemaker.

"What?" she said.

"Just thinking about waking up next to you."

"It doesn't scare you? The commitment?"

"A little, but I still want it."

Her arms tightened. "We can be scared together. And choose to love, despite it."

"You're willing, then? To plan weddings here, even if the Emerson and Halloran names are sharing the title?"

A slow smile spread on her face, true contentment and joy. "I think the Emerson and Halloran names sound perfect side-by-side."

Soft lips landed on his.

He deepened the kiss until she moaned, and his body started demanding nakedness and a mattress.

"What are the chances we could hide away all day without anyone noticing?"

"On Christmas Day?" Her laugh rang across the clearing and out to the lake. "I like your style, but you're dreaming."

He nuzzled her cheek. "There is nothing as rewarding as making you smile or laugh. I could spend the rest of my life working on both those things."

She stilled. "Really?"

The question settled in his gut. It wasn't a hypothetical.

Nor had his statement been an exaggeration.

"Yeah," he said. "Really."

There was that smile again, warming his soul.

"I hadn't planned on proposing today, though," he said. "Suggesting the partnership seemed big enough, and it's fast, and I don't have a ring."

"That's okay."

A ring.

"Wait." He jogged to where he'd left his overcoat and dug around in the inside pocket for the jewelry box he'd jammed in there after winning trivia night.

Emma waited for him at the end of the makeshift aisle. Surrounded by shimmering white and the evergreens and glitter and Christmas and the promise of forever infused within.

Box in hand, he returned to her.

"You *do* have a ring?" she asked.

"The gold ring from trivia night. It's really pretty." He flicked open the top of the box, revealing the simple round stone. "It's an emerald, though."

Her gloved hands covered her mouth. "It's just right. We'll always remember how we fell in love during the holiday season. And on this property, too. I told you this place was romantic."

"You did." He went to kneel.

She caught his elbow. "Don't. You'll get your suit wet."

He lifted an eyebrow. "Are you planning on accepting any other proposals in your lifetime?"

She shook her head. "Absolutely not."

"Then this one's going to be as traditional as they come." He knelt and tugged the glove off her left hand. "Will you marry me, Emma Halloran? Spend our lives being perfectly imperfect?"

She spread her fingers wide, grinning as he slid the ring past her knuckle. "Yes."

He stood and kissed her thoroughly, making sure she knew she was everything he wanted for Christmas. A corny thought, but entirely true. He chuckled.

"What?" she said.

He held her left hand in both of his and rubbed a thumb over the ring. "You're going to have an impossible time trying to find me a better gift than this in future years."

"I'll think of something. I promise."

Touching his lips to hers. "Can't wait to see what you come up with."

Epilogue

One year later

"Better, honey?" Luke rubbed Emma's back, grimacing at the abrupt start to their Christmas morning.

"So much for unwrapping you under the tree." She gripped the edge of their bathroom counter with a hand and rinsed out her mouth. Her sulky reflection was too pale in the mirror.

"Time to take a test, firecracker."

Finally. Her period was almost a month late. She'd sloughed it off, pointing out her cycles were never regular, and she'd been under a ton of stress with Bea's Christmas Eve wedding. Both true things, so he hadn't pushed.

Now that he'd just spent an hour holding her hair back while she retched, he'd push.

Her smile wobbled as she plunked her tooth-brush in the holder on the counter. "Pee on a stick on Christmas? Seems like the last thing we should be worried about. We've got to get back over to the lodge to make sure all the guests checked out okay, and then family dinner..."

Sitting down on the wide edge of their new bath-tub, he pulled her onto his lap and palmed her still-flat belly. If she was pregnant, he planned to spend a good chunk of the next eight or so months hold-ing her.

If for no other reason than it would force her to sit down and take a breath. Between renovations on the main building and the cabin they'd turned into a home and beginning to hold events at the rechris-tened Moosehorn River Lodge, she'd been going full tilt since last January. So much so they'd gotten lazy about birth control during a particularly hectic week in November.

"Emma, you love being prepared. Why are you stalling?" Frustration buzzed in his veins. He was bursting to know.

You know. You're going to be a dad.

"I'm sick of being prepared." She fussed with his chest hair. She'd jolted out of bed so quickly, he was still only in his boxers. "The whole year has been preparations. That wedding was something else. Ours is going to be quiet. Twenty guests, max."

"Whatever you want." He hadn't known how

much chaos a wedding could cause, until Bea Halloran decided to sign up to have her big day televised as part of the newest streaming-service sensation. Excellent publicity for the lodge, but Emma had barely slept in weeks.

She yawned, proving his point.

"I'm so glad we got them married off," he said. "Now I can finally get you to take a nap."

"Shush. *You* need a nap."

"*I'm* not—"

"Neither am I," she grumbled.

"Emma."

"*Luke.*"

Shaking his head, he sifted a hand through her long hair. "So, what's with the prenatal vitamins, then?"

She'd been taking them since the beginning of the month.

"I told you—vitamins are healthy."

"And asking me to deal with the kitty litter?" he prodded. "Taking your bra off the second you finish work because it's too tight? Not drinking at all throughout the festival and the wedding yesterday?"

"I was too stressed to drink."

"Ri-ight." He rubbed a slow circle over her belly. Her pajama T-shirt rode up, and he snuck his hand under, palming her soft skin. "Still feeling sick?"

"No. Just bloated. I couldn't get my candy cane dress done up yesterday. Stupid holiday eating."

"Or—"

"It's *bloat*. Even if I was pregnant—and I'm not—I wouldn't be showing."

"Unless it's twins. Your dad's a twin. Doesn't it skip a generation?" Two-in-one. He wouldn't be surprised. She was, if nothing else, an overachiever.

"It's *not twins*." She groaned. "There's no way. The universe wouldn't do that to me."

"Do—" His throat tightened, and he coughed to keep from croaking. "Do you not want to have a baby?"

"I want to spend my four measly vacation days without having something to worry about. I want to execute our five-year plan without interruption. I *don't want* to wake up and puke every morning for the next two months." Her head lolled on his chest and her lips teased the edge of his beard. "Of course I want a baby. *Our* baby. But—*now*? I had figured year four… *Maybe* three…"

"Shh. Let's see what we're dealing with."

"The night of Bea's cake tasting—we were *not* careful."

Kissing the top of her head, he held her tighter. "I love you."

"I love you, too." She took what had to be the biggest breath in human history and climbed off his lap to mine through the sink cabinet. She pulled out one of the boxes he'd bought and stashed away a few weeks ago. "Give me a minute?"

"Yeah, of course." He went out and sat on the edge of their king-size bed. *Our five-year plan.* Knowing the source of her resistance made it so much easier to breathe. He should have guessed work stress was the culprit.

The minute she'd asked him to start changing the kitty litter, he'd started thinking about their work hours. She couldn't cut back much, not with her growth targets. And being a game warden—certain times of the year, his schedule was all over the place. No good with an infant around, and a busy fiancée.

Fiancée. He'd want to deal with that, too. With one family wedding in the books, he'd get her to move up their own wedding date. She'd intended for the lodge and grounds to be finished before they tied the knot. Waiting until the summer seemed too far off now.

One thing at a time.

The pocket door slid open. She shuffled out, as pale as when he'd left her. She went to her side of the bed and climbed under the covers, pulling the feather duvet to her chin.

He turned, hitched a leg up on the mattress and smoothed her hair off her face. So beautiful, even looking like death warmed over from her first day of morning sickness. *Especially* now. His inner protectiveness was spiking like nobody's business.

Desire, too. Who knew the mere idea of her carrying their child would be so damn attractive? "What did it say?"

"Don't know. I'm going back to sleep. I figure I can wake up, and we can start the day over like we'd meant to. Morning sex. Presents. A quick check on the lodge. Vats of my dad's eggnog."

"I don't think you can have—"

"Don't steal my last thirty seconds of ignorance, Emerson."

Chuckling, he stood and strode to the counter. His amusement turned to a full-on laugh.

Ever covering her bases, she'd taken three tests. They were all positive.

Joy swelled in his chest. Holy crap, he hadn't known it was possible to feel like he was going to explode from sheer happiness.

But everyone adjusted to this kind of news differently. Emma was feeling real fears, and he'd honor her needing more time.

He also had a solution for her that could make things a hell of a lot easier.

Joining her in bed, he snuggled up to her warmth.

"What's so funny?" she mumbled against his shoulder.

"Three tests?"

"And?"

He rubbed his knuckles under the waistband of her flannel pajama pants. "There's a baby in here."

"A zygote," she said, the correction thick with emotion.

"Sure. Still only the promise of life. Call it what you want, honey—if all goes well, we're going to be parents."

Slim arms clung around his neck. "We'll be okay?"

"Yes," he said. "Promise. The five-year plan will work out, too. You'll see."

"How?"

Nerves clenched around his throat. He took a slow breath. "Provided our zygote sticks around, once you deliver and we have a baby in our arms… I'm going to quit my job."

She bolted to sitting. "What?"

"No need to panic. I knew this day was coming."

"When?"

"Last Christmas. After we announced our engagement at the dinner table, and your mom was over the moon about two weddings and who would have grandchildren first. You were trying to point out how your business plans mattered just as much, especially in the short term. I had an inkling then about being the parent at home."

"You *love* your job. You convinced your grandfather to take me on as a business partner so you could *keep* your job."

"No, I convinced him to join forces because I wanted to see you build your dream. I still want that. Being a full-time dad will mean you don't have to compromise your dreams, and I won't feel like a crappy partner and parent because of my work schedule." He tugged her back down. Her heart was beating so hard, he felt it through her shirt.

"Wow. You're actually serious."

"No matter what I'm doing, if it's part of a life with you, I'll be fulfilled." Rolling her onto her back, he rested on one elbow and kissed her deeply. "Merry Christmas, Emma."

"I love you," she whispered, reaching for the hem of her T-shirt and pulling it over her head. Her smile turned saucy. "This time, I'm not going to bolt for the washroom."

"Mmm," he said, dipping his mouth to her peaked nipple.

She hissed. "Careful. They're sensitive."

"Then I'll explore down here."

He trailed his lips over the center of her stomach, resting for a second in the cradle of her hips. *Bloat.* Ha. No way. He knew what her body looked like post-popcorn binge or the all-you-can-eat wing night they still held in the dining hall every couple of months. The fullness under his lips was new, different.

"If it's twins, what do I get?" he said.

"Huh?"

"A bet. If there are two babies in here, what do I win?"

"Uh, a thousand sleepless nights?"

He laughed and tugged her pajama pants down, kissed his way lower until he earned a moan.

"Yes," she said on a breath. "Less talking, more of that."

Mouthing her silky flesh, he murmured, "You know I'm right."

"Maybe." Her hand landed on her stomach, engagement ring twinkling as it always did. She'd been right—it always reminded him of their holiday tumble into love. "Luke?"

"Yeah?" He lifted his gaze to connect with hers. There was need there, and he'd make sure he left her boneless before they got on with their day. But it was the love that bowled him over. Edged with trust, peace, contentment.

Her mouth turned up at the corner, the know-it-all smile forever keeping him on his toes. "Remember last year, when I told you I'd find you a better Christmas gift than our engagement?"

"It rings a bell."

"I think I managed it with twins."

* * * * *

Don't miss the previous titles in Laurel Greer's Sutter Creek, Montana miniseries:

From Exes to Expecting
A Father for Her Child
Holiday by Candlelight
Their Nine-Month Surprise
In Service of Love
Snowbound with the Sheriff

Available now from Harlequin Special Edition!

#2875 DREAMING OF A CHRISTMAS COWBOY
Montana Mavericks: The Real Cowboys of Bronco Heights
by Brenda Harlen

In the Christmas play she wrote and will soon star in, Susanna Henry gets the guy. In real life, however, all-grown-up Susanna is no closer to hooking up with rancher Dean Abernathy than she was at seventeen. Until a sudden snowstorm strands them together overnight in a deserted theater...

#2876 SLEIGH RIDE WITH THE RANCHER
Men of the West • by Stella Bagwell

Sophia Vandale can't deny her attraction to rancher Colt Crawford, but when it comes to men, trusting her own judgment has only led to heartbreak. Maybe with a little Christmas magic she'll learn to trust her heart instead?

#2877 MERRY CHRISTMAS, BABY
Lovestruck, Vermont • by Teri Wilson

Every day is Christmas for holiday movie producer Candy Cane. But when she becomes guardian of her infant cousin, she's determined to rediscover the real thing. When she ends up snowed in with the local grinch, however, it might take a Christmas miracle to make the season merry...

#2878 THEIR TEXAS CHRISTMAS GIFT
Lockharts Lost & Found • by Cathy Gillen Thacker

Widow Faith Lockhart Hewitt is getting the ultimate Christmas gift in adopting an infant boy. But when the baby's father, navy SEAL lieutenant Zach Callahan, shows up, a marriage of convenience gives Faith a son and a husband! But she's already lost one husband and her second is about to be deployed. Can raising their son show them love is the only thing that matters?

#2879 CHRISTMAS AT THE CHÂTEAU
Bainbridge House • by Rochelle Alers

Viola Williamson's lifelong dream to run her own kitchen becomes a reality when she accepts the responsibility of executive chef at her family's hotel and wedding venue. What she doesn't anticipate is her attraction to the reclusive caretaker whose lineage is inexorably linked with the property known as Bainbridge House.

#2880 MOONLIGHT, MENORAHS AND MISTLETOE
Holliday, Oregon • by Wendy Warren

As a new landlord, Dr. Gideon Bowen is more irritating than ingratiating. Eden Berman should probably consider moving. But in the spirit of the holidays, Eden offers her friendship instead. As their relationship ignites, it's clear that Gideon is more mensch than menace. With each night of Hanukkah burning brighter, can Eden light his way to love?

*In the Christmas play she wrote and will soon star
in, Susanna Henry gets the guy. In real life, however,
all-grown-up Susanna is no closer to hooking up with
hardworking rancher Dean Abernathy than she was
at seventeen. Until a sudden snowstorm strands them
together overnight in a deserted theater…*

*Read on for a sneak peek at
the final book in the Montana Mavericks:
The Real Cowboys of Bronco Heights continuity,
Dreaming of a Christmas Cowboy,
by Brenda Harlen!*

"You're cold," Dean realized, when Susanna drew her
knees up to her chest and wrapped her arms around her
legs, no doubt trying to conserve her own body heat as
she huddled under the blanket draped over her shoulders
like a cape.

"A little," she admitted.

"Come here," he said, patting the space on the floor
beside him.

She hesitated for about half a second before scooting
over, obviously accepting that sharing body heat was the
logical thing to do.

But as she snuggled against him, her head against
his shoulder, her curvy body aligned with his, there was
suddenly more heat coursing through his veins than Dean

had anticipated. And maybe it was the normal reaction for a man in close proximity to an attractive woman, but this was *Susanna*.

He wasn't supposed to be thinking of Susanna as an attractive woman—or a woman at all.

She was a friend.

Almost like a sister.

But she's not your sister, a voice in the back of his head reminded him. *So there's absolutely no reason you can't kiss her.*

Don't do it, the rational side of his brain pleaded. *Kissing Susanna will change everything.*

Change is good. Necessary, even.

When Susanna tipped her head back to look at him, obviously waiting for a response to something she'd said, all he could think about was the fact that her lips were *right there*. That barely a few scant inches separated his mouth from hers.

He only needed to dip his head and he could taste those sweetly curved lips that had tempted him for so long, despite all of his best efforts to pretend it wasn't true.

Not that he had any intention of breaching that distance.

Of course not.

Because this was *Susanna*.

No way would he ever—

Apparently the signals from his brain didn't make it to his mouth, because it was already brushing over hers.

Don't miss
Dreaming of a Christmas Cowboy *by Brenda Harlen,
available December 2021 wherever
Harlequin Special Edition books and ebooks are sold.*

Harlequin.com

SPECIAL EXCERPT FROM

HQN

*Angi Guilardi needs a man for Christmas—at least,
according to her mother. Balancing work and her
eight-year-old son, she has no time for romance...until
Angi runs into Gabriel Carlyle. Temporarily helping at
his grandmother's flower shop, Gabriel doesn't plan
to stick around, especially after he bumps into Angi,
one of his childhood bullies. But with their undeniable
chemistry, they're both finding it hard to stay away from
each other...*

*Read on for a sneak preview of
Mistletoe Season,
the next book in USA TODAY bestselling author
Michelle Major's Carolina Girls series,
available October 2021!*

"Who's dating?" Josie, who sat in the front row, leaned
forward in her chair.

"No one," Gabe said through clenched teeth.

"Not even a little." Angi offered a patently fake smile.
"I'd be thrilled to work with Gabe. I'm sure he'll have
lots to offer as far as making this Christmas season in
Magnolia the most festive ever."

The words seemed benign enough on the surface, but
Gabe knew a challenge when he heard one.

"I have loads of time to devote to this town," he said solemnly, placing a hand over his chest. He glanced down at Josie and her cronies and gave his most winsome smile. "I know it will make my grandma happy."

As expected, the women clucked and cooed over his devotion. Angi looked like she wanted to reach around Malcolm and scratch out Gabe's eyes, and it was strangely satisfying to get under her skin.

"Well, then." Mal grabbed each of their hands and held them above his head like some kind of referee calling a heavyweight boxing match. "We have our new Christmas on the Coast power couple."

Don't miss
Mistletoe Season *by Michelle Major,*
available October 2021 wherever HQN books
and ebooks are sold.

HQNBooks.com